MUSEUM
of the
AMERICAS

STORIES BY GARY LEE MILLER

Fomite
Burlington, Vermont

The following stories have been previously published, some in slightly different form: "Museum of the Americas," in *Hunger Mountain;* "Killing Houdini," in *Green Mountains Review;* "The Truest Curse," in *Chicago Quarterly Review;* "Winter," in *Gray's Sporting Journal;* "Certain Miracles," in *Washington Square;* "In His Condition," in *The Florida Review;* "Benefits," in *Miranda;* and "Into the Rushes," in *Atelier.*

ISBN-13: 978-1-937677-78-7
Library of Congress Control Number: 2014940307

Fomite
58 Peru Street
Burlington, VT 05401
www.fomitepress.com

Cover and interior design by Joanna Bodenweber
Author photo by Carley Stevens-McLaughlin

For my sister Carol

Thanks

Many people supported me in the creation of this work, and I would like to give them my most sincere thanks. They include my teachers: Douglas Glover, Diane Lefer, Pamela Painter, Ellen Lesser, Steve Almond, Christopher Noël, Syd Lea, and Rick Simpson; my Vermont College family: Tom Miller, Sandra Miller, Lisa Carey-Miller, Po Powers, April Ossmann, and Rich Farrell; The Arlington Writers' League: Bob Dall, C. D. Collins, Karen Roehr, Liz Buchanan, and Holly LeCraw; my most excellent friends David Redmond, Peter Drescher, Ken Tonnissen, Nat Winthrop, Craig Snyder, Holden Smith, Rob Madrick, and Joseph Tovares; and the entire population of Eldred, PA, the most magical home town on Earth.

Most of all, I would like to thank my family. In the bar rooms of northern Pennsylvania, my father, Earl Miller, taught me how to tell stories. My mother, Dorothy Miller, never lost faith in me, even when I lost faith in myself. Maddie, my daughter, saved my life and changed my world in the best of ways and forever. Eli, my stepson, proved to me that unexpected circumstances sometimes lead to great happiness. And Deb, my life partner and my first and best reader, helped me understand that no matter what we have or don't have, life can be beautiful. With all of you on my side, how can I lose?

CONTENTS

Museum of the Americas

The Museum of the Americas hasn't had five visitors a month since 1973, when they put the interstate through and left this part of the Upper Valley like a rock in the river that's too far to reach from shore. Admission is three dollars, which doesn't add up to much. I live off the money Dad left from the Museum's glory years and try to run the place the way he would have if he were still alive. Dad was a master of the tourist business, and I hold hard to his principles, because that's what he taught me, the one of his two sons who wanted to learn.

Once every few weeks in the summer, visitors stop by, people who remember the Museum from the years before, or who make a wrong turn and decide to take a look before wheeling around in the gravel and dirt parking lot and moving on to where they'd intended to go. A couple pulled in last Thursday, the hottest, driest day of the year, in an old clay–colored Chevy wagon with Illinois plates and a little blue–and–white Scotty camper tagging behind. The woman drove, which seemed funny for people my age, better than seventy and with their best years behind them. She pulled the little rig into the Museum lot and it petered to a stop, barely stirring dust.

"What kind of exhibits do you have here, mister?" she said. Her voice was firm and honest, and I couldn't help but like it, try as I did not to.

I could have answered as simple as she asked, but that's not the way in roadside attractions. "Soil," I said, just like Dad would have, a little hum in my voice, a little shill. "We got soil from Tierra del Fuego to Tierra del Alaska, and all the Americas in between." I smiled, to give her that welcome feeling.

The man slept leaning up against the window and she tapped him on the arm. "We're here," she said, as if they came here on purpose, instead of by accident. This got me to thinking about the old days, before the interstate spoiled it all.

WHEN Dad dreamt up the Museum of the Americas in 1949, just two years after my mother died, the whole family thought he was crazy. We had milked Holsteins through the Depression and nearly starved, but with the War, things had been steady. Dad's pitch was that steady wasn't enough. A new breed of cow gave milk better than any Holstein. The tourist.

Dad turned the words on his tongue like a schoolmaster as we sat at the dinner table, him and me and my older brother Kenny.

"Tourists'll mean more to Vermont than milkers ever have," Dad said, "Milk you can make a penny off of. But a dimwit from the city can make you a dollar."

We didn't believe him, Kenny especially, who was fifteen then and in the middle of a long career of battling with Dad.

"People are gonna drive all the way from Boston to see a museum on a farm in the middle of Vermont," Kenny said. "I most doubt it."

Dad didn't say a word then. The dinner table was sacred, a place where peace was guaranteed, even to Kenny. But later that evening I heard the beating, and took it as a sign of our doom.

It turned out, of course, that Dad was right. He had powers—not just the power to throw bales of hay onto a wagon all day long in the summer sun, but powers Kenny and I could never imagine having for our own. Dad knew. He dreamed those cars nudging their way into the Upper Valley like calves to the teat, and people with more money than we'd ever seen, and his dream came true. Before long, visitors started driving to Vermont from Boston and New York and Saratoga Springs and Hartford, and the locals who waited at the edge of the road with something to sell never lifted another shovelful of cowshit in their lives.

THE woman from Illinois climbed out of the wagon and went around to her husband's side, pulled him up out of his seat as his faced soured with pain. Having to be helped embarrassed him. I saw that, and looked away. Dad trained me to watch visitors, take action to please them in any way that didn't cost money or break his rules. He'd smile, chat with the men about the trout fishing, compliment the ladies on their hats. He'd dote on the children especially, in a way that made me work harder to please him. And when I'd done right, the small reward that came, a nod, maybe, or a squeeze on the shoulder, made me feel special, that's all. I learned to love that feeling.

The man in the pickup gathered himself upright. I stepped toward him and held out my hand.

"Colonel Bill Davis, USMC, retired," the man said. "And this is my wife, Norma." The Colonel wore creased khaki pants and a khaki tee-shirt and loafers, a gray brushcut and tobacco-brown skin, tattoos faded to the color of mold. His handshake was soft, although he tried to squeeze. There had been more to him at one time, but sickness had worn him down.

"Tom Grant," I said. Norma held out her hand and I took it. Her thin hair had more lead to it than gold, but her pale blues eyes and the blush to her cheeks made me think she must have been beautiful some years before. She wore khakis like her husband's, a blue cotton blouse, and small red canvas shoes with white laces. She smelled of old fashioned perfume.

"We heard about this place," she said. "But we didn't half believe. We been on the road since daylight Monday, and we haven't had our dinner yet—"

The Colonel cut her off. "We came a long way to tour your museum," he said. "If you don't mind, we'd like to get started."

Norma stood looking at her shoes.

"It's not a matter of whether I mind," I said. "We closed twenty minutes ago. Hours are ten to five."

You might think me cruel. They'd come so far and him sick. But the Colonel wasn't the first pushy visitor I'd seen. "Give a tourist an inch and check for your eye teeth," Dad used to say. "They'll take 'em and your molars to boot."

I saw my brother in the Colonel's face then, the look Kenny got when he'd run into trouble and didn't understand why. Kenny never got the point—that sometimes you do things just because you should—and he still doesn't. He mostly drinks, and works on the engine of a Chevy or a Ford when he runs short of money for liquor.

I'm not rebellious. A few good beatings taught me to do what's right. So it surprised me to find myself considering something Dad would not have approved of. The look on the Colonel's face, that quiet hurt, softened me somehow—or made me bolder.

"I'll make an exception," I said. "Once. On account of how far you've come." I tried to sound stern, but I couldn't help letting some kindness leak into my voice.

"Bless you," Norma Davis said, but as she spoke I heard Dad, too, calling me an idiot, saying this was trouble. Even in the heat, I shivered.

THE Museum of the Americas doesn't look like much from the outside. A long, low-slung clapboard building, more of its washed-out yellow paint peeling than not. A sagging cupola with a cast-iron bell and half a dozen pigeons nested in. As we walked to the entrance, the Davises peered down the length of the ratty old place, and I saw disappointment in their eyes.

The Colonel pulled out his Zippo lighter and lit up a Pall Mall.

"You know you shouldn't," Norma said.

He ignored her, and she turned my way.

"Emphysema," she said. "They've told him he won't last long if he keeps this up."

The Colonel took a slow, deliberate drag, exhaled, took another and tossed the cigarette into the dust. He coughed roughly and spat, wiped carefully around his mouth with an old white handkerchief.

"The sign says three bucks," he said. "Is that it?"

I nodded.

His hand shook as he passed me a ten dollar bill. I counted change from my own wallet and gave him two red paper tickets, each torn in half.

I pushed open the door and reached in to switch on the lights. As we stepped into the room, a cool draft reached out to meet us, and the scent of good, sweet earth tumbled softly down the back of my throat. In my mind, I heard the old man's words, and I took a deep breath and spoke them like he taught me, not too loud to be irritating, and perfectly clear.

"The building is set sixty inches below ground. The main exhibit is at normal basement level. This allows for natural cooling and helps to preserve the soils."

The Ball jars sat row on row, freshly polished, brass lids winking, the varnished pine shelves giving off a separate, ambered glow. Inside the jars, heaped two–thirds of the way to the lid, not compacted but held loosely, "to breathe" as Dad used to say, in shades of sulfur and rust, powdered cocoa and cast iron, were the soils of the Americas.

"It's beautiful," Norma Davis whispered. People often do.

IN the beginning, the Museum of the Americas had more standard exhibits, mostly Indian artifacts Dad bought at auction. A Mohawk mask and some arrowheads. An old tom–tom and some antlers tied together with a deerhide thong. Three months after the Museum opened, just as business was starting to pick up, one

Professor James E. Erickson came up from Harvard University on a day when Dad wasn't around, and he talked Kenny into selling all of those things for a hundred dollars. My brother was honestly trying to please Dad. I believe that. But Kenny didn't stop to think how much those old Indian things were really worth, or that they could make us more money in the long run if we kept them around.

I will never forget the whipping Kenny got. I lay in the dark in my bedroom listening, and the worst part came when he couldn't cry any more, and there was only the sound of the strap.

The next morning, Kenny stood at the breakfast table because he could not sit, his food untouched and his face changed somehow, as if he knew something the rest of us did not. I turned away from my father as he spooned oatmeal onto my plate. Dad took it as a challenge.

"You go ahead and sulk, Thomas," he said. "But my job is to teach you things that you'll never forget, by example or by other means. Do you understand why your brother got hell?"

I looked at Kenny, and more than anything I wanted to help him. But through his tears I saw what he was. Someone who begged for sympathy when he'd done something he shouldn't, but would go right back and do wrong again the next chance he got. I, on the other hand, was the good boy, the boy who was learning to run the Museum of the Americas. Like my father, I had the place in my blood.

Dad set a glass of milk beside my oatmeal.

"Well, Thomas?" he said.

"Yes sir," I whispered. "I understand."

Quietly, Kenny began to cry.

Without the Indian relics, the Museum of the Americas fell back on the only exhibit it had left. Soil. You'd be surprised how many people drove out of their way and paid good money to see it. Of course, this wasn't just soil from the back yard. It came from Jasper, Alberta and the Yukon and the Alamo. There was soil from Bolivia and Guatemala and from the digging of the Panama Canal. I'm not sure how Dad got all of it, how much he paid. Every so often a package came, peppered with stamps and heavy for its size. The Museum of the Americas might be your only chance to see Colorado River silt from the Grand Canyon of Arizona or black gold from the cotton fields of the Mississippi Delta. People lined up at the Museum door summer after summer.

THE soil in the first jar was pale and sandy, mixed with bits of purple and black. The Colonel read out loud from the history thumbtacked to the shelf below the jar. "Soil of the Eastern Woodlands Indian. From the shell middens of the Wampanoag, raised up at their gatherings before the coming of the White man. Taken at Corn Hill, Truro, Cape Cod. May 13, 1950 by Custer A. Grant, Curator.

"Look around," I said, feeling Dad's voice in my throat. "I'll gladly answer any questions that you have."

I'm shyer than Dad was, quieter, but I do a good job. I picked it up quick, got into the routines, did what I was supposed to and didn't do what I wasn't. And I couldn't help thinking how easy it might have been for Kenny, if only he could've brought himself to do the right thing for once. Why people take the hard road is a mystery to me.

The Davises moved quickly down the row of shelves, hardly bothering to read the histories, which are what make the Museum interesting, if you ask me. "Soil is where life comes from and where death goes to," Dad used to say, "and what man walks on in between."

They finished the exhibits on one side of the room, and moved to the other. By the time they were halfway along the wall, their smiles were gone. Holding hands, they passed down the line, slower and slower until they got to the last exhibit, soil

7

from the Falkland Islands that a British soldier sent from the war. They stopped and stood.

"Mr. Grant," the Colonel said. He took a weary breath. "Is this all you have?" He stood at parade rest, his hands clasped behind his back, his feet spread slightly apart.

"Yessir," I said, irritated. "Soil. I told you that before you came in."

"It isn't that," Norma said. Her voice sounded hopeless. "Do you have any more samples besides the ones on the shelves?"

"Oh Lord, yes," I said, feeling dumb. Dad never squawked when I made a mistake with a visitor, but he always knew.

"We're interested in something particular," the Colonel said.

"Yessir?"

"Soil from the jungle. We wondered if you had that, Mr. Grant. From the Amazon. From Brazil."

"Yessir," I said. "We have Amazon soil," and I recalled Dad saying how people go for the exotic over the ordinary every time. It took me a minute to find the jar, high up on a shelf in the back, the soil black as India ink, a spiderweb of moisture creeping up the inside of the glass.

"That's the stuff," the Colonel whispered. Norma came forward into the little room; all three of us crowded together amongst the dusty shelves and bottles, beneath a single yellow bulb.

Slowly, the Colonel's hand squeezed the rim of the jar. He struggled for breath, and after a snap of his wrist that I could almost hear, the lid began to turn and rise, scraping softly against the spiraling ridge of glass.

And then the smell. The Colonel lifted the lid and it poured out, rich and wet and full with life. "Hmm," he said, and Norma and I said it back. We stood there for a moment, and I closed my eyes, the wonderful smell of that soil filling me, and then I heard the lid slowly spin closed.

The Colonel sat the jar back down on the shelf. He looked

straight into my eyes with his own, resolute and honest.

"What would you take for it," he said. He nodded at the jar.

I answered him the only way I could. "I wouldn't take anything. It's not for sale."

"Just tell us what you want for it," Norma said. "We'll pay."

I cleared my throat. Most people would have gotten the point, but the Colonel went on.

"It sure would mean a lot to us, mister," he said, in the kind of wheedling tone that a man of his stature shouldn't use.

"Didn't you hear me?" I said. "I won't repeat myself." I shut off the light and closed the storeroom door.

They followed me out silently, and we all stood for a moment in the sun. Just when I started to feel embarrassed about the harsh way I'd spoken, the Colonel asked if they could camp in the parking lot for a couple of days before moving on. Dad wouldn't have done it, but the guilt moved me.

"That's fine," I told the Colonel. "Two nights, but no more."

That evening, as the dark came on, I spied on them from the kitchen window. They brought a lantern, a folding table and chairs out of the camper, set up a gas cook stove and soon I could smell some kind of a stew. The lantern hollowed a honey-colored space out of the night that seemed to be made for just them. They were making my place into their own. Dad would have considered it black sin.

EARLY the next morning, Norma Davis knocked at the back door. I opened it and she stood there, holding a plastic pail. Beyond her, I could see the Colonel, sitting on the Scotty's wrought-iron doorstep, smoking a Pall Mall in the already slaking heat.

"I'm sorry to bother you," she said, "I was wondering if I could get some water from your outside spigot."

"Sure," I said. "A dollar fifty a bucket is what I usually charge."

That was Dad talking, but before I could take it back, she dug six quarters out of her snap change purse. I walked around the house and turned on the spigot. It ran slow, and I stood near her while the bucket filled, looking up the valley for a sign of rain.

"It's not just for ourselves that we want that dirt. It's for our boy. Daniel."

"It doesn't matter," I said. "Because I can't sell it. My father left it in his will that way, and I can't let any of it go." Purely speaking, this was a lie. My father trusted that I knew what to do with his legacy. He did not have to write things down.

"When he turned eighteen, Daniel joined the Corps," Norma went on. "It was his father's idea, mostly. The boy finished boot camp and took his thirty day leave. He packed up and went on a vacation to the Amazon.

"For two weeks, we didn't hear a thing. Then it was four weeks, and his return flight came and went. We got a letter, saying that he wasn't coming back. I seen it comin', but Bill, he didn't. He promised never to forgive the boy, and he hasn't. Even after we got the letter sayin' that Daniel was dead. It's been twelve years, now."

"So your husband wants something to remember your son by."

"There's more to it than that."

Water flowed over the rim of the bucket, staining the dry grass dark.

"We were sent here," she said. "Because Bill's dying."

"A jar of dirt won't cure emphysema."

"I know it," she said. "Bill always wanted to travel out West, and with his condition, we figured we better do it soon. In Tucson, on the street, we met this Indian. He said he was a seer, and I wouldn't have believed him, but he proved it. He knew us, somehow, knew about Daniel and Bill. And he knew this place. He sent us, Mr. Grant. He said Bill should steep a tea from that Amazon soil and drink it, and he'd have peace over Daniel, and Daniel peace over him. So we got in the truck and came here."

When I was a boy, we had our God. He raised his temple and charged visitors by the head and sat across from us at the dinner table and said Grace. "If God blessed us, what did Ma die for," Kenny would say, and Dad would beat him to a rag. And a week later, Kenny'd say it again, and get the same.

"Listen, Missus," I said. "This is a museum, nothing else. It can't straighten out the mistake your son made, no matter what some medicine man says."

"You never knew Daniel, Mr. Grant," she said. "What makes you think he made a mistake?" She took up her bucket and walked toward the Scotty, the water where it spilled raising tiny explosions of dust.

THAT night, rain threatened. Thick, hot bolts of grit-laden air rattled the bedroom windowscreens, and I lay on my bed for hours, trying to sleep. I closed my eyes, and a vision of Dad emerged from the darkness. He stood at the entrance to the Museum in his creased black trousers and his starched white shirt, his back straight with pride, and I heard the joyful timbre of his voice, the love, even, for what he had built there, as he spoke to a group of visitors, led them inside. He turned toward me and I could not face him, and then he turned away.

The telephone startled me awake at a quarter past three. I pulled on some dungarees and a shirt, flipped on the hallway light and went down to the kitchen.

"Tom," a man's voice said.

"Yessir."

"It's Jim Fletcher at the State Police barracks at Harrisville. We got Kenneth over here. Driving under the influence, same as last time, no accident, nobody hurt. He says he wants you to come down and pick him up."

From the window, I saw the Scotty trailer, its tiny windows dark and its painted steel skin glowing softly in the moonlight. The Davises were sleeping, dreaming that the Colonel could drink a tea of Amazon soil and be shed of his agony, of what his son had chosen and done. But a life is not that easy to change, whether it's your own or somebody else's. It involves work, and you can't go begging for miracles.

"You just hang onto him," I told Jim Fletcher. "He knows better than to have you call here, and for all I care he can sit there for the rest of his life." I slammed the receiver down into its stirrup and went out onto the porch to get some air.

THE breeze had died and the heat risen again, but I smelled water; it came from nowhere in the dusty heat. I turned and walked out into the yard, wondering if I tasted the first wisps of a rain, but the storm had blown over, and the stars shone clearly against pure blackness, and not even the most distant glimpse of heat lightning paled the sky.

Yet around the doorstep, the air hung like clean, wet bed-sheets, just pinned to the line. It seemed like nature had moved out of turn somehow, and I might have gone to bed believing that, strange as it was, but then I noticed the sound of water hitting earth, and I realized that the Colonel's wife had been at the spigot again and left it partways on. Dad was right, and he had always had been. People would take advantage; people were selfish, inconsiderate, and small.

I was halfway across the parking lot before I could stop myself. I jumped on the corrugated steel stoop of the trailer and hammered on the door, echoes loping back and forth across the lot, from the trailer to the Museum of the Americas and the rocky hills beyond. The camper leaned on its keel, and the door tilted open. In the doorway stood Norma Davis, draped in an old cotton robe.

"Turn on the light," I said. Blood churned in my eardrums, and my skin burned hot.

"Mr. Grant," she said. "My husband is sleeping."

"I do not give a God damn. I want you off my property, and I do not want to wait until morning for that to happen. Turn on the light."

Norma switched on a battery lantern, creating a pale yellow dome of illumination that left smudges of blackness at the high and low corners of the trailer. I saw clean dishes stacked beside the sink, a tiny table piled with clothes. The lantern's reflection shone in the pail of water that sat on the trailer floor.

The Colonel slept on a bunk folded down from the wall. I could hear his faint breathing. He lay covered in a blanket, and only someone dying could be cold on a night like this, but that did not lessen my anger or bring any shame.

"I heard your phone ring," Norma Davis said. "Late night calls often mean trouble."

"There is no trouble," I answered. "Other than that I have made myself, against my better judgment."

"I wish you wouldn't talk so loud," Norma said. "We'll leave in the morning, like I told you, and we don't mean to bother you at all."

"But you are bother," I said. "There is nothing else to you but that."

"I paid for the water," she said sullenly. "I left the money inside the door."

"I do not want your money. I want your departure."

"You'll wake him," she said. She moved farther into the doorway, as if to push me out. But I was on my own land, and I knew the rules.

"Waking your husband is my intention," I said. I considered

hitting her then, to get her to step back, but I saw movement in the back corner of the trailer, heard bedclothes rustle, and I stopped myself. The deck of the trailer shifted once more.

The Colonel slowly rose up on his elbows. His hair stood at angles to itself like a stormbeaten hedge. He poked around on the night table for his eyeglasses and a dry cough came, a convulsion, and the eyeglasses clattered to the floor. He blinked and stared in the cobwebby light.

"Danny," he said to me. "Son, is that you?"

Once more, I recognized my brother in the Colonel's face. But this time, I saw just a bit of the real Kenny Grant, a person who had made mistakes—not on purpose, maybe, but because he was human, plain and simple, because he came from earth and would go back to earth and, and in his hurry to live in between, might act without thinking something through the whole way. And then I understood. It was not up to me to give salvation, or to withhold it. It was not up to me to judge.

Dad would never have forgiven what I was about to do. "Stay until morning," I told Norma Davis. "But that's all. I don't like people on the property. That Museum door has never been locked. And I don't expect to start locking it now."

"We're not thieves," she said.

"I didn't say that. It's just that with me asleep, you could get into that storeroom and take whatever you wanted. I don't mean that you would. But the opportunity presents itself. Do you understand me, Mrs. Davis?"

She smiled and began to thank me, but I hushed her with a look.

"Be gone in the morning," I said.

She closed the camper door.

DAD always said that for every night a visitor camped, you'd spend two days cleaning up after him. Yet this once, it seemed,

14

he was wrong. When I woke the next morning, hardly a sign of the Colonel and his wife remained; even the Scotty's tracks in the parking lot had been taken by the wind. It was afternoon before I noticed the visitors had left something behind. The Ball jar leaned over on the grass near the spigot. Soil of the Amazon Basin, the label read. Collector unknown. A tiny puddle of water, no more than a tablespoon and speckled with tiny flakes of soil, lay in the bottom of the jar.

I picked the jar up, unscrewed the lid, and put my lip to the rim. The scent that rose was not of the Amazon, but of the entire history of my life. Cowshit and dollar bills, visitors from Boston and New York and Saratoga Springs and Hartford, raised welts and Dad's dinner table, betrayal and fear.

I swirled the water around for a minute, watching the particles of soil drift, spin, and collide, moving in courses beyond their control. Then I tipped the jar upward and drank. The water felt cool and sweet on my tongue.

Winter

From the kitchen window, the old man looked across the yard to the plywood hutch at the edge of the hayfield where the dying setter was tied. The kitchen was warm and dark, but outside, in the isinglass-tinted November air, an occasional snowflake rocked slowly down, settling, blooming for a second and melting on the hard, cold patch that the dog's rope kept raked down to dirt. The Agway thermometer nailed to the porch post outside the window read thirty degrees. It had fallen steadily since daylight, when the old man rose from his bed in the corner of the kitchen and made a new fire in the woodstove. On the radio, they called for snow. It wouldn't get cold enough for her to freeze to death—that would be a blessing of a kind—but the snow would make it harder for her to get around. He could bring her inside, but she'd be unhappy there; all her life she'd lived for the scent the wind carried. He'd made her a bed of straw inside the house he'd built from old barnboard; she'd be snug in there, but she'd dropped ten pounds or better, and slept more than she was awake, even in the daytime. There was nothing left for her but suffering, and it was time for that to end.

He'd noticed the tumor weeks before, stopping by her hutch on the way to the shed to get the lawnmower. The first snow had yet to fall, and the last of the turned leaves still held on to the row of oaks behind the tractor barn, but he could smell cold earth and leafmold. He looked into the upper field and thought about the pheasants stretching and scratching between the rows of corn stubble and wondered if the setter might want a go at kicking some out for him later toward dusk. When he stepped within the radius of her chain, she trotted to him, put her front paws on his hip and bucked her muzzle against him for attention. He scratched the underside of her jaw and she yelped, dropped, and cowered on the dirt.

"Hey, now," he whispered. "Hey, Vera, honey," And he coaxed her, shaking, into the crook of his arm, slid his old, split fingertips gently along the liver–speckled slack of her throat. He shuddered when he came to it, solid, big as the pit of a peach. "If it ain't this," he whispered, and took his hand away from the lump, pressed his papery lips onto her muzzle. She smelled old, familiar, like clothing someone near to him had worn, and he held and stroked her for a long time, his rough hands passing again and again over her mottled white fur.

Cancer was something the old man knew. His wife Elizabeth had died of it three years before, after the doctors had taken every part of her body that could be taken, shot her full with every kind of drug and radiation they could find. He had just the farm and the setter now, and the farm was almost gone, the last of the Herefords butchered when Elizabeth was sick, for quick money to pay the hospital and the doctors, most of the acreage gone fallow. An auctioneer put the tractor and the bailer and the hayrakes and hand tools on the block, but most of the equipment was outdated and little of it sold. He advertised the barn for scrap lumber, but found no takers.

Even without the farm producing, the old man got by. The house and land were paid for, and he drew a veteran's pension. Karl App leased the upper field for corn and hayed part of the rest, paying for what he got at a dollar-fifty a bale. The old man couldn't hold onto a car at that, and he walked into Martin's Bridge once a week or so and carried back groceries in his trapping basket. Every three weeks, the Agway brought 50 pounds of feed for Vera. It ran him extra for delivery, but the dog was what he had. There had been no children. Hands were hired on and off with the seasons, the last one gone the autumn after Elizabeth died.

AT half past nine, with high, coal-colored clouds gathering above the timber lot and the cornfield, he took the setter out a pail of water and a cookpot full of Blue Seal feed. He'd used to throw bales in the hayloft or onto a wagon all day long, but now even this small weight was enough to strain at the couplings of his wrists and elbows. He was getting skinny; his green work pants puffed out around what was left of his legs, his ancient Pendleton wool coat draped across his shoulders with no more definition that it would have had on a wooden hanger. As he stooped and set the water and feed down at the edge of the bare dirt, his thin gray hair stood up against the wind.

The bunch on her throat had bulged up her jaw toward her muzzle, and she no longer ran hard to the end of the rope; she sidled over now, stepping daintily, as if the ground were some kind of fallen bird that she did not want to ruin. Her appetite had lessened, and the feed bowl was nearly full. The old man whispered to her quietly and held the food to his own mouth to show her how delicious, dipped a handful of pellets into the cold water and tried to coax them past her lips. She tilted her head slowly sideways and raked a few of the corn-yellow stones in with the curl of her tongue, rolled them around and around in her mouth and chewed carefully, as if she nursed a bad tooth.

When he tried to feed her more, she held her muzzle closed, as if the old man's attempts at feeding her were some tired and regular inconvenience, she walked to the hutch and entered, her tail thumping its walls as she turned on her straw and lay down. "Son of a bitch!" the old man said. He flung the cookpot toward the hutch, and it hit with a flat clank, the feed pellets bouncing off the frozen ground like hailstones.

The old man turned and studied the house. Fractured shafts

of sunlight pierced the hard gray clouds above the ridgeline and angled down onto the tin roof, long gone of paint, the posts of the porch slowly sinking through the ripening floorboards. All of it was going that way. The barn had partially collapsed in a summer storm; rotted planks at the west corner splayed out from the foundation like straw from a broken bale. The house, although better built and looked after, had not seen attention in many seasons, and would follow.

At first he'd railed against the aging of the farm, fought it with paint and new shingles, silvery spools of barbed wire, but as every season turned, he saw more clearly how natural the decline was, and he fought it less and less. The smaller outbuildings disintegrated first. The wooden taps he'd driven into the oldest maple trees were grown over with new bark or rotted; above them dead branches hung, waiting for the wind. The lower fields, left unplowed, showed the ordinary succession of growth that planting and harvesting denied, and his own body weakened, grew stiffer, and moved toward the same end as the stalks of milkweed along the fencerows. The best he could hope was to shepherd the fall until he became part of it. This he accepted. But to do it alone was not what he wanted, and although the dog was the last thing that kept him from that, he understood that her dying was as necessary as that of the ancient maples in the dooryard, as the barbed-wire fences' rusting away, opening the pastures to whatever new lives would have them.

Three days earlier, he'd gotten as far as loading up his .22, sitting at the kitchen table while he did it, his back to the window. It took him half an hour to get a shell into the breech of the gun, another twenty minutes to stand up and push back the kitchen chair. He'd stopped at the screen door. It was a perfect day for hunting birds, the sky tall and blue and hard, the leaves scattered on the sharp green of the yard like shards of broken varnish. Vera lay in front of the hutch, sleeping, the warm

Indian summer breeze lifting the tufts of her fur. She'd hear his footsteps, and when she saw the gun, she'd rise and come out to him, despite her sickness. The long, feathery arc of her tail would sweep the air and she'd nudge as hard as she could against the end of the rope, longing to bury her nose in the leaves and discover the scents of grouse and woodcock, eager for the point and the sharp smell of burnt powder. If it had been years ago, when he had hired help on the farm, one of them could've shot her. But he couldn't do it himself. He unloaded the .22 and put it back in the cabinet.

This wasn't the first thing he'd done. After finding the tumor, he'd called Rupert Holland, the vet who'd cared for the old man's animals for as long as he'd run the farm. A young man, whose voice he didn't recognize, answered the phone.

"Your grandfather there," the old man said.

"No," the voice said. "He isn't." There was some kind of accent to it; couldn't be any of Rupert's people.

"This the vet's office," the old man said.

"Yes sir, it is. Lee Carlisle speaking. How may I help you?"

"My setter's got a tumor on her throat. Big as a man's thumb, about. A little more. How much will it run me to get it took out?"

A dull click brushed the old man's ear. "Could you hold, please," Carlisle asked. "I've got a call on the other line."

While he waited, the old man thought about trying to bring Vera inside, where she wouldn't have to worry about the weather. That made him smile. The other dogs he'd owned had tried to sneak into the house every chance they got, but Vera wouldn't come at all. Refused. In the blizzard of 1972, Elizabeth begged him. "She'll freeze, Kenan. Go out and drag her in." He still had the scar on his forearm where the setter bit him as he tried to carry her through the door.

He chalked it up to her being a bird dog. A good hunter's nose would find little in the house to enjoy—even less since

Elizabeth died. He'd moved a cot in and lived in the kitchen, unable to afford heating the whole house, uncomfortable with its emptiness. So the kitchen smelled like a man's place. Hair oil, tobacco, cough syrup, and dust. Woodsmoke and fried eggs. Outside, Vera got the scent of grouse and pheasant, fox and coon. When Elizabeth was dying in Porter County Memorial, her nostrils filled up with medicine and cleaners, the conditioned air that wasn't air at all, she begged to be brought home. "I need to smell the farm again," she said, and although the doctors told him that there was no way she could stand the travel, he came with the truck and carried her there. "I want to be outside," she said when she woke up the first morning, and he put her in the wheelchair and eased her out onto the porch. Summer was just coming on. Starlings lined the fencewires by the road, and the sky was warm and blue. "I believe," Elizabeth said, "that I can smell the corn starting to leaf out." And she closed her eyes.

"HELLO?" Lee Carlisle said. "Are you still holding? You had a problem with your dog?"

"Yessir," the old man answered after a second, surprised to find the phone receiver in his hand. "Vera. Rupert knows all about her. He give her all her shots, fixed her after she had her third litter. He's hunted behind her, too. Tell him she ain't doing so good. Or if he ain't busy, I'll talk to him myself."

Carlisle was apologetic, professional. "Doctor Holland no longer holds the practice. He retired two months ago."

"The hell he did?" That was news, but not a great surprise. Rupert had practiced far longer than most probably would have. "Oh. So you took over, then?"

"No. I'm Doctor Brady's assistant. I'll be glad, to look through the appointment book and see if we have a visit available for you and your animal, Mister -"

"Kenan Hakes. Vera's the dog. Animal. Hakes, too, I guess

you'd say." When, he wondered, did things get so god damn formal?

"We can book you in December 18th."

"She's too sick for that," the old man said. "I seen tumors on a dog before."

"Well... I could ask Doctor Brady about an emergency call, but that would be extra. He's really busy this month. Rabies is moving up from West Virginia and he's booked with inoculations all over the county."

"Do what you can," Hakes said, "But she's in rough shape. How much will it run, do you figure? If I can get in?" The wooden box on top of the refrigerator contained twenty-four dollars, all he had until his next check came in. That would've been plenty enough for Rupert.

"Well, it's hard to say," the assistant answered. "Depends on how far along the tumor is. Is she eating and drinking?

"She drinks, but she don't eat much. Sleeps, mostly."

"Is she uncomfortable most of the time? Howl or whine at night? Any fits or seizures?"

"No. But she just—"

"Well. It sounds like she's fairly comfortable at least. Might even be a benign tumor, although with the eating dropping off, I doubt it. The office visiting is sixty–five, the biopsy might be as much as two–fifty, depending. It could be that -"

"How much to put her to sleep?"

"Oh. That would be sixty. But you'd still have to wait for that first appointment. I'm sorry, Mister Hakes. There's Dr. Allen in Collinsport. He might be able to fit you in. Do you want his number?"

"No," Kenan said. "I can't haul her that far. You call me back if you get an appointment. If not, I'll take care of it myself."

THE old man went to the window and checked the Agway thermometer. Twenty-eight. The cloud cover would keep the temperature from dropping much lower, but the snow was picking up, and the big flakes fell regularly, like they were dropping from a conveyor belt, sticking to the hutch and the dirt patch in front of it like petals of lace. The chickadees had swarmed the bittersweet bushes the evening before, stuffing themselves with the bloodcolored berries, and hadn't come back. The wind had shifted and came out of due west, clanking the wooden chimes hanging from the roof peak, rattling the back door screen. The storm would be a big one, and there wasn't any way he could leave her through that kind of weather.

He went from the window to the narrow, dusty stairway, up through the dark to his and Elizabeth's abandoned bedroom, found the string to the light switch, and pulled. The drawn white windowshades threw back the light, and the musk of old bedclothes pressed onto his tongue. He opened the gun cabinet and took out the .22, tucked a paper box of cartridges into the pocket of the Pendleton coat. The door of the gun cabinet creaked oddly as he closed it, and a sound that mimicked it rose in his throat. He struck at the light string three times before his grip held, and then he stood in the darkness for a moment, dizzy, as if he were standing at the edge of a mineshaft.

The floorboards of the porch sagged when he stepped onto them. At the sound of the closing door, Vera rose. It had begun to snow harder now, flakes as big as nickels slanting uniformly down, their aimlessness driven into order by the increase of the wind. Perhaps it was the thickening snow, perhaps it was that the disease had already begun to take her eyesight, but he reached the edge of the bare dirt before she noticed the gun. She whined and slowly swung her tail.

"Hey, Vera girl. Hey there." He crooned it as languidly

as he could, the syllables snagging in his throat. "Hush, now. Hsssssh."

A twenty-foot length of bruised white clothesline rope connected her to the hutch. His knee joints burned as he squatted, undid the hutch end of the rope, wrapped it twice around the palm of his canvas work glove, and stood. Vera shook the snow off her coat and sneezed, broke into a lope but stopped short of the lead's end and walked, her moist breath spuming out onto the air. She took a nose toward the hickory grove in the low place behind the barn, where they usually looked for grouse, but he whistled her back. "Wrong way. Come on," he called, and when she turned and leapt toward him, he saw her for a second as she had been before, hoped that he had imagined her sickness, but she reached his side breathing heavily and limping, as if that much of a run were all she could take. The old man stepped from the yard onto the dirt driveway, head down, rifle under his arm, following the soft, fringed impressions her paws made in the snow-confected mud. He turned at the main road and looked back, but the house was lost in snow. "Take a right, Vera," he said. He switched the rope gently and she turned.

WHEN they reached the Colebert house, he stepped up onto the porch and tied the rope to the wooden railing. An inch or better of snow had gathered on his collar. When he took off his wool hunting cap, it tumbled down the back of his coat and wet the spot between his bony shoulder blades. He rang the doorbell, then, unsure of whether the bell was working, tapped hesitantly on the aluminum screen door. The setter, near exhausted, lay on the porch floor, her paws dangling loosely over the top step, her ribs heaved out against her coat like the coils of an old, heavy spring.

Young Jim Colebert answered the door. He was tall and skinny, with a small paunch nudging at the front of his flannel shirt, dark hair combed back and lightly oiled, wire–framed glasses with tape at one bow. His eyebrows gathered at the center of his forehead when he saw the old man. He looked at the snow that huddled on the stairsteps and the dog stretched out on the porch, the long sweep of her tail sprayed across the painted boards like a fan. He looked at the gun.

The old man recognized Lynnette Colebert's voice. "Jim? Who is it? What do they want?"

Colebert turned and hollered over his shoulder. "It's Kenan Hakes." He turned back to the doorway. "Keen. Good Lord. Come in. Did you two get lost or something? Come in. Are you all right?"

"I'll stand out here," the old man said. He felt as if the weight of the snow on his clothes was enough to take him to his knees. "I'm OK. But Vera ain't." He nodded at the dog, waited until he could speak again. "She ain't good at all. I need you to help us out." He looked at the tall man's face.

"Let me get my boots on." Colebert stepped inside the door and closed it behind him. While he waited, the old man tried again and again to look at the dog, but could not bring himself to turn and face her.

Colebert came out onto the porch, his blue jeans tucked into his black rubber barn boots, an orange wool watch cap pulled over his ears. He moved past the old man and squatted on his haunches next to the dog. She raised her head and sniffed. "She don't look hurt," Colebert said, standing up and turning toward Hakes. "What'd she do, step in a chuck hole?"

"We wasn't hunting," the old man said, holding up the rifle. "She's full of cancer, and I can't stand to see her suffer no more. I brought her out to shoot her, but I can't do it. I want you to do it for me."

Colebert stood, looked at the rifle. "Why not take her to the vet?"

"Rupert don't practice no more. The new fella wants sixty dollars to do it, and he's busy besides. Can't take her for two weeks at the earliest. I got twenty-four dollars I'll give you for it. I'm sorry, but it's all I've got."

"I won't take your money, Keen. I can't shoot no dog."

"It's a hard thing," the old man said. "I tried to do it myself, Jim, but I just couldn't. She's a good dog, Vera. Hunt? Hunt like hell. Isn't a dog in three counties like her." He took a pack of Luckies from the Pendleton coat, shook out two cigarettes, and held one out to Colebert. "Smoke?" All around the porch, the heavy snow fell, and the wind carried it through the trees with a sound like waves.

"Sure. Just don't tell Lynette."

The old man clinked open the lid of his father's Zippo and lit his Lucky, then Colebert's. He snapped the lighter shut. "This here," he said, holding up the rifle. I'll give you the Marlin. I don't use it no more, but it's in good shape. Seven shots with the clip, and I got a four power scope for it at home. I'll throw that in."

"I already got a .22. The boys got me one for my birthday two years ago. And it isn't that..."

The old man's face was flushed. "Well, maybe they'd want it, then. When they come home for Christmas. Come to think of it, I got half a dozen muskrat traps I could give you. Victors. Number one and a half. I'd throw them in. And I might even have a few stretchers on top of that."

"It's not that, Keen. I don't want to shoot her."

The old man ignored him, held out the gun. "She always liked to hunt that field up beyond your barn. I'd like to bury her there. If you'll help me with that, too, I'd appreciate it." He stepped closer and pressed the rifle into the younger man's hands, held it there, until Colebert took its weight. He looked at the dog, still curled up on the porchboards, a dust of snow settled on her coat, then back at the old man, and stopped fighting. "I just want to go tell Lynnette," he said, "and then I'll take Vera out back of the house. You want to wait inside? There's coffee on."

"I'll take her out there myself," the old man said. He undid the rope from the porch railing, and the dog stood up. Together, they walked slowly down the snow-covered steps.

He wondered at how long it had been since he'd visited the Coleberts, how much Jim Colebert's face had aged. When Elizabeth was still living, there had been friends come to dinner, parties at the holidays. After she went into the hospital, people brought him food and company and he returned it when he had the time. But when Elizabeth died, his want for company fell away. He found that the farm was all he needed, the house and the barns and the weather, the things and the memories that Elizabeth had left behind, his shotgun when he wanted to take a walk, the dog to keep him company. Through one season after another, he had lived his life alone.

By the time Colebert came out through the back door of the farmhouse, the old man had untied the rope and knelt next to his dog in the snow. He held her for a long time in his arms, even after Colebert came out, rubbed her fur and cooed into her ears and kissed her forehead again and again, as if that could prevent the pain of the bullet's entering. When he stepped back, she took a step after him, and he told her again to sit. Colebert held the .22 under one arm, a blue nylon blanket and an ash–handled mattock under the other.

"I'm ready," the old man said.

"I'm not."

"Well. Take your time. She'll sit as long as I tell her to, and I told her." The old man walked to the corner of the house and looked out toward the barn, a gray shadow on the screen of whiteness below the heavy black clouds. A minute passed. Two. The dog whimpered.

"God damn it," Colebert said. "I just can't." He coughed. The old man stood, unmoving.

The heavy curtain of snow insulated the report of the .22 to a dull pop, and it was not until Colebert ejected the shell that the old man opened his eyes. The blanket, unfolded, lay strangely on the snow, disrupting its whiteness. Colebert leaned the gun against the porch post and walked over to pick up the dog. "Wait," the old man said. "I want to help you."

They lifted her onto the blanket and folded it over, used it like a stretcher to carry her up to the field beyond the barn. She was a fair-sized dog, and it took some time for Colebert to dig the hole. The old man helped him cover her over. By the time they finished, it was almost black dark.

"Do you want a marker," Colebert said. "I got some two by twos in the barn."

"I don't believe so," the old said. "It wouldn't last anyway, with the weather."

The snow was up past their ankles, their shoulders covered in white as they walked back toward the farmhouse. "I can't let you go back on your own, tonight, Keen," Colebert said. "And I can't drive you back there, either. We'd just end up in the ditch. This storm is supposed to keep up all night."

The old man paused, stepped carefully over a fallen log. "I got here walking," he said. "I'll walk back." In the side pocket of the Pendleton coat, his hand squeezed the coiled piece of clothesline rope. The soft, waxen gutters of his face were brimful with tears.

They broke from the field into the yard of the farmhouse, the rectangles of yellow light cast out into the cascading snow, the warm, dry smell of woodsmoke from the chimney pressed low to the ground by the storm.

"Lynnette's planning on having you to supper," Colebert said. "By the time we're done eating, there'll be snow up to your knees. You can take one of the boys' old rooms."

The old man stopped at the edge of the house and looked across the fields toward his farm. The fire would be long dead in the wood stove, the dog's hutch layered with snow, the house standing black and lifeless in the middle of the drifted fields.

"Well hell, Jim," the old man said. "Twist my arm. I'd never hear the end of it if I turned her supper down. But I'll be out as soon as I can in the morning. I got work to do up to the house."

"All right," Colebert said. "As soon as the plows come through, I'll drive you up." The old man followed him up the back steps and through the door, to the warmth of the wood-stove, the dinner on the table, a place by the door to hang their coats.

The Truest Curse

My mother, Adriana Balnavera, was a full time Advisor. That's capital "A," as in palms and Tarot, and the future only the Gypsy knows. We had fourth-floor rooms half a block down from the Boston Common on Townsend Place, with an upturned palm of anemic pink neon in the window that one in a hundred people might notice. My father, João Pareces, was not a Gypsy, but had been a crooked policeman in Lisbon and had good business sense. He'd tried to talk my mother into putting a sign at street level where people could see it better, but she'd refused.

"They will find me when they need me," she'd said, laying her accent on heavy like she did for the Gadjo, the white-skinned Americans who came to her for Advice. "True power does not need cheap advertisement."

"Bullshit," my father answered, but the Gadjo came. It was the most accurate prediction my mother ever made.

In 1968, I was fourteen years old. For two years, since getting my "moon blood," as my mother liked to call it when the Gypsy Urges seized her, I had been an Advisor. I read palms for five dollars and tarot for eight. All the money I took in was "turned over to the family," meaning my mother, who dispensed it as she pleased to my father, my little brother Bento, and me. My aunt Thessa lived with us too, but was independently wealthy, courtesy of a back injury sustained behind the wheel of her cherry-red Ford Falcon convertible and a weekend job at the Filene's jewelry counter.

I kept the money I earned in a mayonnaise jar behind the sofa, saving it for my getaway, when I'd escape my mother and her Embarrassing Gypsiness forever. Every day, I watched from the apartment window as the soot-skinned Greyhound buses wheezed past the corner, leaving the Arlington Street station for anywhere but here. I imagined standing at the ticket booth with enough sweaty dollar bills in my hand to pay my way to New York or even California. But what I really wanted couldn't be bought. I wanted to be an American Girl. I knew the world they lived in existed; I'd seen it myself on television, and I wanted to live there, too. But to do that, I'd have to stop Advising, stop being Gypsy, and that, according to my mother, was impossible.

"You are Romany, and you can't change that," she told me. "The Gypsy is inside you, Mirena. If you want to throw it away—you can try. I've seen people do it. And what do they get? A cursed life. So you want that?"

In 1968, it seemed like much of life had already been cursed. Every night at six, the grownups huddled in the kitchen around the tiny Sears black-and-white television to watch Walter Cronkite's news. As they smoked João Pareces' Portuguese cigarettes, buildings burned in the cities of America and people died in Vietnam. Bento and I, in the living room playing nickel-ante poker, listened as the comments drifted out from behind the kitchen's curtained French doors.

"The Gadjo should know that they can't keep the dark-skinned people away from their fate," my mother said one night in July, when it was so hot and humid that even the walls of the apartment seemed to sweat. "Why don't they just bring their soldiers back here and let Vietnam be?" Fate was something Adriana Balnavera talked about often, and when she did, it usually took her side.

I shuffled the cards and dealt to Bento, who picked them up in his small brown hands and studied them as if they contained the mysteries of this life and the next. After a minute, he pulled one card from the hand and lay it face down on the dirty beige carpet. I dealt him another card, and he pushed three nickels into the pot.

Outside on Townshend Place, car horns trumpeted and tires squawked on the pavement. In the kitchen, gunfire rattled from the television speaker. After it had stopped, Aunt Thessa weighed in. "Just be glad that you have only one son, and that he isn't old enough to fight. Sons are the truest curse. They start out like angels and grow up to kill the world."

My mother, who generally supposed men to be dishonest, unfaithful, and useless, agreed. But my father insisted otherwise. He hadn't drunk a drop for over fifteen years, but he'd learned his philosophies on the barstools of romantic Lisbon. "The truest curse," he pronounced, "beyond a doubt, is love."

Adriana answered this with a string of obscenities, but Thessa just laughed, a high bubbly sound I loved, because it meant hope. Outside this apartment, people lived in big houses with swimming pools. They drank Coca Cola, and went on vacation to Disneyland. Inside the apartment was Mama, and her aura of permanent gloom.

Why she couldn't be more like Thessa, I never understood. They were sisters, born in the same place and only a year apart. But it was as if one had absorbed all the good lessons of the world, and the other all the bad. Thessa trusted everyone, my mother no one. Thessa gave and my mother took. Thessa talked to me, listened to me, paid me attention with small gifts and sidelong glances, with small touches of her tiny, ring-bangled hands and kisses on my forehead. My mother bossed and bullied, measured out doses of affection so small and infrequent that the last one was nearly forgotten before the next one came. A hand on my shoulder as she worked in the kitchen, kisses so seldom that I longed for them until my skin ached.

As much as I hoped for a change to come, I knew it probably

wouldn't. The Advising business, and the money it brought, stole my mother's attention from me. Vietnam was turning America upside down, but war wasn't always a bad thing for an Advisor— in 1968, more Gadjo visited us than ever before. Girlfriends, wives, and mothers came to see my mother and me, to look for the fortunes of their soldiers, as the women of soldiers have always done. Soldiers rang our tinny doorbell, too, the bravest and the most afraid. They tiptoed up the long, dark flights of stairs and gazed into a future that my mother and I uniformly presented as murky but leaning toward the positive. "It isn't fair to show them a perfect fate," Adriana told me before I read my first soldier's palm. "It would make them careless. Fate has no love for careless men." It was one of the few time I heard her say anything kind. But the visitors brought money with them, too. And if anything could open Adriana Balnavera's heart, it was dollar bills.

Soldiers for peace came to visit us as well. Except they usually came for a different reason—they hoped to change the future of the world. Drugs and gurus got most of the attention in those days. But Advisors played a part, too, helping the peace soldiers get away from the blood and the pain, predicting that a better world would come soon.

My mother had little good to say about these teenage boys and girls, who swarmed like iridescent beetles on the Boston Common during the warm months, drumming, dancing, smoking hemp, and shouting about the war. "They're money, that's all," she said. "Money and nothing more. If they weren't rich, they'd have to join the army like the poor kids, and maybe they'd make something of themselves."

Aunt Thessa took a different view. She admired the peace soldiers, not for their money or their war protests, but for their fearless abandon, the wild way they lived.

One morning, she and I passed by a group of them on our way to Inman Square, Cambridge, where we shopped once a week at the Portuguese markets for the groceries we needed: black-roasted coffee and cigarettes, linguica, figs, and salt cod. Shopping with Thessa was one of the few ways I could escape the apartment even temporarily—and only because she'd sworn an oath to keep me away from the Gadjo—and Gadjo boys especially. But I had eyes, and Thessa knew it. As we passed the Common that morning, she slowed the Falcon to nearly a walk, ignoring the drivers that swerved angrily around us, leaning on their horns. It was early morning still, and the Common was mostly empty. But a dozen kids gathered near a boy who stirred a steaming pot set up over a Coleman camping stove. He wore a long, intricately-patterned skirt knotted at his bony hips and a black tee shirt above, his rust-colored hair cinched up into an explosive tangle with strips of yellow cloth.

Thessa tucked a fresh Viceroy between her lips and spun the wheel on her Zippo lighter. "Look at them, Mirena," she said between puffs. "They don't give a care about nothing. Every morning when they wake up, they decide who they're gonna be. And halfway through the day, if they want to be somebody else, they do that, too. You want the truth, if I was young like you, I'd be out there."

As we passed by the end of the Common, Thessa picked up speed and turned her eyes to traffic. Quickly, so she wouldn't notice, I waved at the tangle-haired boy, my heart crashing against my ribs. The boy saw me; I knew it, but he didn't wave back. I was Romany, after all, and a stranger to almost everyone.

IT was just a few days later that the girl named Chloe visited us for the first time. My brother Bento brought her, having spent the morning handing out Adriana Balnavera's business cards on the street. ("Advisor to the Seventeen Courts of Europe. Knows All. Tells All.") The doorbell jangled four times, the signal for a customer, and the click of Bento's Buster Brown shoes echoed up the stairwell, another set of footsteps after them, lighter and more delicate. The sounds grew louder, rising on the hot, humid column of air, and then the footsteps stopped outside and Bento tapped gently on the door.

Fanning herself with a magazine and fussing with her hair, Thessa humped her way across the room, the flared legs of her mint green pantsuit swishing as she moved. She slapped back a baroque collection of deadbolts, and the door leaned open on its own. The doorway stood empty for a long few seconds before Bento stepped into it, his sunbrowned hand attached to one nearly as small, but fairer. The girl followed reluctantly, Bento tugging her arm.

"Welcome," Thessa said. "Please come in." Bento scooted for the kitchen; his job was done, and he could rest a while before heading back out to the street.

The girl stood in the doorway, adjusting her eyes to the dim light.

"Raven wants me to check this place out," she finally said, speaking to no one in particular. She swung a thick bank of loam-colored hair behind one ear and gave the room a long, slow look. She was a peace soldier; I could tell by the patched denim bellbottoms and stained red velvet vest she wore, the handmade bead bracelets on her wrists and the scent of smoke and sweat she carried into the room. She looked about my age, but she had matured more quickly, and I saw my father behind the French doors, eyeballing her curves and her soft, narrow waist, the tanned skin that showed around the borders of her vest. Her face wasn't perfect; her chin was too stubby and her cheekbones too flat, but her lucent, bottle-green eyes startled me, made me hate the both of us for what we were and weren't. I would never be that pretty, and I knew it.

"What do you want," I said, with more of a challenge in my voice than I'd intended.

"Raven says there might be answers here."

My mother, who had been listening from the kitchen, swept into the room, nudged Thessa aside and took the girl's hand. Adriana Balnavera found mothering to be foreign, but could pretend it to advantage when necessary.

"Raven?" she said. "You are girlfriend?" I lowered myself into the armchair across the room, ten feet of cheap pile carpet between me and my mother's Hollywood Gypsy accent. I wanted to disappear, to be anywhere else at all, but I knew that leaving the room would be a mistake.

"I'm Chloe," the girl said. "And I guess I'm his girlfriend." She smiled shyly, and my mother leaned over, took the girl's stubby chin in her palm, and tilted Chloe's greeneyed face toward her own.

"I know this," my mother said, "just as I know that you have many difficulties together, you and this boy."

"Not everything is bad," Chloe said, her voice growing quieter, less sure. "Some things are cool. But this one thing isn't."

Adriana took her hand away from the girl's face, walked slowly toward the middle of the room and the table where we did our Advising. A Tarot deck lay there, and she slipped a card from it. Pressing the card against her tiny bosom, she walked to the window and stood there, looking toward the heavens, as if waiting for a sign. "Three o'clock tomorrow" she intoned, without turning around. "Bring this Raven here then. And tell no one else. Keep your secrets and keep them well." The window show was Adriana's favorite trick, and she did it because it worked. She stood with her back turned until Chloe disappeared down the stairs, as quietly as she'd come.

THE next afternoon, we all sat in the kitchen, waiting for Raven and Chloe. As three o'clock approached, my mother began to talk about how she could use their problems to her advantage.

"Knowledge. Deep knowledge. That's what they want," she said in a voice that wavered in the timbre between hatred and contempt. She was skinny, much skinner than old Gypsy women are supposed to be, and her hair was thin and warped with gray, but her fat, tennis-ball ankles made her look solid, somehow, impossible to push over or around. She leaned down to massage them as she spoke, grimacing at their complaint.

"Now, Mirena, look at your father. Sitting all day smoking a cigarette, never working, while you and I make the money that feeds this family. Do you think that if I had any deep knowledge, I would have picked him?"

My father laughed a very small laugh and popped a bit of smoke from his acne-scarred cheek. He leaned back in his chair and drew his brow tight. "Let me see, now. Why, Mirena? Why do you suppose?" He winked across the kitchen and I giggled.

The truth was, he'd met my mother while arresting her on the docks in Lisbon, where she worked providing favors to lonely sailors. It was an old family story, and we all knew it well, even Bento. But it had lost none of its power over the years. Adriana crushed her cigarette in the big glass ashtray and leapt from her seat.

"You know that the charges were false. The whole world hates the Gypsy. But they always come to us." She whirled toward me and extended a long, twiggy finger, dipped in red nail polish and adorned with sculpted silver rings. "They think they want some kind of secret knowledge, but what they need is hope. Someone to tell them that their future is bright. And that, Mirena, is what you'll do."

My mother spoke the truth. What most people need when they come to an Advisor is what they already have. They want to be told that the life they are living is normal and that their troubles will some day come to an end. And that's what the Advisor tells them. But they leave thinking that they've gotten something more—a certain glimpse of the future. And that's the trick that keeps the Gypsy in business.

Calmer now, Adriana eased back into her chair and held out her arms. I stepped toward her and she pulled me onto her lap, stroked my short dark hair. What she planned for the Gadjo wasn't exactly honest. But for a rare moment, everything was different, and I was in my mother's arms. Adriana had birthed me, and she was supposed to love me. And there was one thing I could do for her that just might make her do that. I closed my eyes and curled up into the hollow of her neck, feeling a secret joy.

It was ten after three when the intercom buzzed. The boy came in first, with Chloe behind him.

"Is the medium here?" He stressed the word, as if it were important for me to hear that he knew it.

"It's me." I felt the words shake out, as if I were suddenly jerked up by the ankles and forced to look at the world upside down. I had never seen a boy so beautiful. His skin was bare from the waist up. His thick, smooth muscles lay tight along his bones. His feet were bare as well, and I could not avoid looking at them. They were something I wanted to touch.

Raven walked directly to the card table and sat. He moved like a wild animal, smooth and sure, ready for anything. I tried to take a step toward the table, but my feet wouldn't budge. My mother saved me, rushing from the kitchen to put an arm on my shoulder, pressing me forward and into the chair opposite him before retreating to the kitchen.

"Sit down." I said to the girl. She sat. "I can see that you are here because of a problem you have." Chloe nodded. Raven gave her a scowl that he thought I didn't see. The scowl that said "Hey. Don't give her any clues. Let's see how good she is on her own." I had to suppress a smile. That was the easy one. Anyone coming to an Advisor has some kind of problem.

I pointed to the boy. "You want to start first?"

"Yes." For a moment, I dangled by my feet again.

"Palm reading is five dollars," I said. "Tarot is eight. Each. Do you have the money?"

There was a small silence, then Chloe reached inside the waistband of her flowered skirt and took out a dirty five. "Just him." She started to hand it to me, then dropped it in the center of the table, embarrassed. Again Raven scowled.

"Thank you," I said gently, trying to make her feel more relaxed. And to him, "Your hand."

The heat wave had continued, lading the apartment with a tangible steam, but his hand felt cool to the touch. I slid my fingers along his wrist, felt the pulse there as my own quickened. Trying not to shake, I turned his hand palm up. His lifeline, the only one most Gadjo expect, was long. I told him, and he rolled his eyes.

"Raven!" Chloe's face lit with anger, and in that moment, I saw she was more beautiful—and stronger—than I had realized. She was equal to his power in some ways, if not in all.

"No," I said. "It's all right. He hasn't done this before." It was a guess, but a good one. The doubt vanished from his face.

I continued, tracing the lines on his palm with the tip of my index finger. I had done this dozens of times, and had never felt anything special about the contact of my skin against another's. But now it was different. I felt a tingling on the surface of my skin, a rising of nerve, which spread from fingertip and radiated to my stomach, the base of my spine. Did he feel this too, I wondered, then shamed the thought away. I closed my eyes for a moment, breathed as slowly as I could until I was calm enough to speak. When I opened my eyes again, he was there, beautiful and waiting, his dark eyes wide and mirroring mine.

"This problem," I said, "is becoming more and more complicated."

Chloe took in a breath, and I followed it.

"Do you see this line? The one here with many smaller lines from it?"

"Yeah," Raven said.

"This line shows me that the problem exists. These small lines, I am not as sure. Someone else involved, perhaps. Or more than one way to solve it."

Chloe's eyes filled with tears. He pulled his palm away from me and lay it over hers.

"Shhhh," he said. "Shhhh. It's OK, Clo. We're all right."

When I was preparing to become an Advisor, my mother once told me something important. "There are times, Mirena," she said. "When you have to take chances in order to earn your keep."

"Stand up," I said to Chloe. "Come around the table."

She moved slowly, uncertain of what might come next, then stood stiffly in front of me, terrified, as if I was about to cast a spell from which she would never be released. I held up my right hand.

"Take my hand, Chloe," I said, "and put it on yourself.

She took me in both of her hands; I felt the heat and moisture as they pressed against my own. She paused a moment and tears lost their grip on her bottom lashes and fell, flattened against her cheek. She pressed my hand tentatively against her belly.

"How long, Chloe?"

"Ten weeks," she stumbled through her tears. "Twelve. I don't know." Suddenly, Raven stood behind her, crossed his muscular arms over her chest and pulled her against himself. The contractions of her crying lessened, and she sipped a long, slow breath. I took Raven's palm in my hand and turned it upward, looked at it for something that would tell me what to do. I saw nothing there; the story was in Raven's eyes. They showed that he understood what he'd done, that he wanted to do something to help. But he also wanted to escape.

The three of us stood there, our skins touching, our blood beating in our veins, and for the first time, I understood my power. With a few words, I could change their lives forever. But the power held me prisoner, too. No one could free me from the choice I needed to make.

I let go of Raven's hand, walked to the window and looked down on the street. The cars flowed past on Townshend Place, every one headed to somewhere I wanted to go. As the cars streamed past, I counted to myself slowly, as my mother had taught me to do. When I reached fifty, I spoke to them without turning around.

"Come back tomorrow, at exactly the same time. I'll have answers for you then."

That night, I lay on my blanket on the living room floor where all of us slept, the table where my mother and I gave Advice pushed to the side of the room. The pale silver bloom of the streetlamps slipped in through the Venetian blinds. I opened my hand and tilted it toward the window. Where the bars of light lay across it, my palm glowed as if lit from inside. There were more lines than I had ever noticed; running parallel and intersecting, smaller ones feeding larger ones like rivers to a stream, tangled in each other, yet in perfect order. They were the maps of my future but I had no idea how to read them.

My father rolled over and groaned, rose to his feet and walked toward the back of the apartment. I heard the sound of his water trickling into the toilet and the low moan of the building's ancient pipes when he flushed. His footsteps tread quietly back toward the front room and then stopped. I rolled over and looked toward the kitchen. The doors hung open, and I saw the shadow of his body, leaning over the countertop next to the tiny kitchen stove. I heard the click of Thessa's Zippo and a tiny blue flame popped to life. He dipped his cigarette in the fire, then the lighter clicked again and the flame vanished. I lay on my pillow and watched him as he smoked, the glow of the cigarette revealing the lines and creases of his dark Portuguese face.

My parents had been married for more than twenty years, and while I knew the story of my mother's arrest, I'd never heard the part that came later—how they fell in love. There was me, my brother Bento, the wedding bands on my parents' fingers, so it must have happened. It was no use asking my mother. Fate was how she explained almost everything. But what did fate mean? Had she and my father no choice about meeting and falling in love? Could nothing in the world have changed that? And if fate ruled love, what did it mean for Raven and Chloe? What did it mean for me?

I closed my eyes and let visions of Raven wash over me, the smooth cords of muscle along his collarbones, the slender white scar along the curve of his upper lip. I tried to recall the way he'd looked at me when the three of us touched, he and I with Chloe between us. I had seen something, I was certain, directed at me. Just how did the curse of love begin?

After a few minutes, my father coughed and mashed out his cigarette, shuffled his way to the front room and lay down next to my mother. She rolled over in the half-light and folded around him in her sleep.

THE murmur of voices woke me. It was my mother and father in the kitchen, she drinking coffee and my father scrambling eggs with chorizo; I could smell its peppery, greasy scent drifting into the living room. Thessa had gone out already, on her weekly trip to the car wash on Broadway in South Boston, and taken Bento along.

"The two Gadjo, they'll fatten up our pocketbooks," Adriana said. "Mind me, João. Poor kids don't run away like that; they don't have the money to live in the park all summer. Poor kids go away to fight the war."

"War?" my father said. "He's too young. Fifteen, sixteen.

In the old days, the Army would take him. But not any more."

"Maybe so. But he's got the money; I can smell it. And he's old enough to get his daddy to open his purse."

My father's long-handled spatula scraped the cast-iron fry pan. Plates clucked together on their way from the cabinet, and the smell of the peppers grew stronger.

"You'll only see money if the girl can convince him to get it," João said. "She's got her nose full of him, you know."

"Of course she does. She's knocked up. She's scared to Christ."

João chuckled. I pictured him slouching in front of the stove, shirtless, an unlit cigarette clamped between his tiny yellow teeth. "Who says I was talking about his girlfriend?" he said.

I pulled my rust-stained cotton bedsheets over my head.

"What," my mother said.

"I said 'if the girl can convince him,'" João said, "I didn't say anything about his girlfriend. It's Mirena that's got her nose full of that boy. Maybe you didn't see it, but I did."

"Mirena? My Mirena?" Adriana laughed louder, and my face bloomed hot. Her footsteps thudded toward the living room.

"Mirena?" The footsteps stopped beside me; through a gap in the sheets, her Gypsy ankles loomed.

"Mirena! I know goddam well you're awake, so don't try to pull no shit on me."

She bent down and yanked back the sheet, leaving me huddled in my cotton nightgown. I fought to force the blood away from my face as she circled me, her voice rising like steam in a kettle.

"Is what your father said true? Do you want to love a Gadjo? Do you want to take your clothes off for that rich Gadjo boy? Tell your mother, and tell me the goddam truth."

I shook my head.

"Tell me, you filthy puta! You father saw it. Either he's a liar, or you are!"

I rolled up from the floor and dodged her swatting hands,

sprinted to the bathroom, and locked myself in. She hammered the door and shrieked, alternately spat curses and begged me to undo the lock.

Inside the bathroom, I pulled my clothes from the cardboard box that served as my bureau, got dressed, and when I heard silence, opened the door. The weak heart that my mother died of was inside her then, and she leaned against the doorsill, panting like a hound.

"Mirena," she said, her voice as close to weakness as I had ever heard it, "Look at what this has done to me already. You can't make love to the Gadjo boy. It would kill me. His parents would never have you, and you'd end up like that other poor girl; pregnant with no place to go."

I didn't know how to answer. The thought of Raven's baby inside me made me dizzy.

"Mirena?" Adriana said, louder this time, but less angry, pleading more than demanding. "Do you hear me?"

I nodded.

"And you will stay away from this Gadjo boy?"

"Yes."

With a surprising spring, she snatched me by the hair, snarled her rough hand in it, and yanked my face toward hers. The blood in her face had warmed her perfume to a thick vapor that caught like burnt sugar in the back of my throat.

"I will stay away!" I shouted, and she released me, coughing so hard it seemed as if her rib bones might snap. At last she finished, emptied out like a cornhusk doll. In the silence that followed, my father called in from the kitchen.

"Don't worry, Adriana," he said. "She'll stay away from him. Like the she cat from the he."

RAVEN and Chloe didn't show up that day—or the next. I paced at the windows, feverishly studied my palm, trying to discover the reason they stayed away, trying to envision when they'd return—or if they would—but the lines revealed only my limitations as an Advisor, and my future stayed hidden.

Enraged that their absence cost her money, my mother tilted through the apartment like a drunken mule, sucking cigarettes and spitting curses. "You look at the boy too hard!" she yelled at me, over and over. "The girl can tell. They won't come back, and it's all your fault." I begged, cried, and promised repentance, and when she cornered me, spat back curses of my own.

On the third day of my mother's tantrum, Thessa came to my rescue, sweeping me away on a shopping trip in her Ford Falcon. She'd invited me for a reason, and she knew why I'd accepted; she steered the naugahyde jewelbox of a car through the narrow streets of Chinatown with a knowing smile, not speaking until we'd rolled onto 93 North, spinning smoothly toward the spender's paradise that was tax-free New Hampshire. A light rain fell, and a fog pushed its way over the low, rocky ring of hills north of the city. The cozy slap of the windshield wipers and the hiss of the rain beneath the wheels made me relax for the first time in days.

"I didn't tell your mother what I saw about him," Thessa said finally. She lit a cigarette, tilted the rearview mirror to check her Gadjopolitan hairdo, and, dissatisfied, cursed gently but effectively in Romany. I turned toward the window and watched the fogbound landscape slide past.

"The boy has feelings for you as well," she continued. "Not love, perhaps, but feelings. Did you notice that, Mirena?"

My face burned.

"What Adriana said about his family might be true also. It probably is. You have power over him, but not over his rich mommy and daddy. Could you live without his money, if you just had him?"

I turned from the window. "Thessa! Do you think I'm like

Mama?"

Thessa laughed, fussed with her hair some more, pulled a curl down over her dark eyes and watched with satisfaction as it sprang back into place. She pulled me closer to her on the seat and put her arm around my shoulder. "No, Mirena," she said. "I think I'm right. Your feelings for that boy are true."

"But what about the girl?" I said, and Thessa squeezed me tighter.

"You're father's correct, you know, about the curse of love. It's the worst of all, but sometimes we forget. For every love that exists, someone is happy. And someone is ruined. Do what's right, Mirena. You'll know what it is."

WEEKS passed, of tracing my palm and waiting for Chloe and Raven to return, of holding my breath against the future and hoping it would finally come. Slowly, rubbed against reality, the hope began to smudge away. Other Gadjo came and went, satisfied with their fortunes, at least as far as I knew. By the end of August, I'd given up; I'd never see either Chloe or Raven again. But then, on a Sunday in the first week of September, the boy came back to me, alone.

My mother, my father, Thessa and I were sitting in the kitchen watching the morning talk shows; Bento had already left for the street, a clutch of my mother's business cards in his hands. The doorbell rang only once, loud and long.

My father got up to answer the door. "It must be Mac," he said, heading to answer the bell. "The dogs been running good, and he wants me to go out to the track." But I knew it wasn't Mac, or any of my father's friends. My palms told me; the lines on them began to tingle, then to burn. I tried to concentrate on the television, where a woman was showing how to bake some kind of cake, but then I heard Raven's voice. Before my mother could stop me, I was at the French doors, easing one open just enough to peek into the living room.

"I'm here to see your daughter," Raven said. He wore a white shirt with a collar, gray corduroy slacks, and white leather sneakers. He'd combed his hair—or maybe Chloe had done it—and tied it with a leather thong.

"Oh?" my father said, as if maybe he didn't have a daughter, and the boy had come to the wrong address.

"Mirena."

"That's fine. Palm or Tarot? My wife does the Tarot, also, if you want."

"Neither," Raven said. I squeezed my palms together, and the heat between them became almost too much to bear. "But I'll pay, if I have to. I just want to talk to her. That's all."

My mother reached to grab me, but I slid a chair between us, and before she could say a word, I pushed open the doors. What started in confidence quickly turned into fear—three steps into the room, and I was dangled by the ankles again, terrified and helpless. My voice abandoned me, and the room spun. He stepped toward me and I pointed at the table. He pulled out a chair and sat.

The Tarot deck lay on the table in front of him. My hands shaking, I spread the cards into a fan, tilted one up with my fingernail, and took it. I walked to the window to gather some air, pressed the card against the screen, afraid to look at it and, finally, afraid not to.

The delicately watercolored woman, dressed in flowing robes and holding two shining broadswords crossed before her, was turned head downward. My mother herself had taught me the Tarot, and I knew what this card meant—betrayal and trickery, deceit and bad advice. Even a Gypsy couldn't stop a card like this one.

Thick, heavy air pressed through the windowscreen, and then the tiniest tongue of a breeze came, the first cool tendrils of a storm, scuttling drinking cups and newspapers down Townshend Place, lodging them against its granite curbstones. I felt the thunder first, then heard it, watched as the storm's first huge drops pattered the newspapers to the ground. The rain fell harder, and on the far side of the street, a young woman left the fender of a parked car and moved gracefully into the shelter of a doorway. Chloe. It had been only a month but her shape had begun to change; she was visibly maternal, even at a distance. She saw me; I knew that, and knew that I held her fate in my hands as surely as I held my own.

I pressed the Two of Swords against the windowscreen, waited until the soothing breath of the rain cooled my burning palms. My heartbeat slowed, and I took a breath. Held it. Let it out. Took another, and decided. My eyes on Chloe, I cheated the card, rotated it to place the sword woman right side up. When the card stood upright, another meaning was true: harmony and courage, restoration of peace. I turned from the window, walked to the table, and sat down.

"You didn't come back when I told you," I said to the boy. "Maybe it's too late. Maybe I can't help you any more."

Still, he smiled. The perfect sculpt of his throat thrilled me, the juncture where his neck met his jaw.

"Mirena," he said, and that thrilled me, too, to hear him speak my name, "I need to talk with you."

"I know," I said. I closed my eyes and breathed, then opened them again. "It's five dollars."

He dug five ones from his shirt pocket, pushed them across the table, turned his palm up and lay his hand in my own. The heat rose in me again, and I wondered that he could not feel the burning. I took another breath and began, saying what I needed to say, though all of me fought against my tongue, trying to keep from saying it.

"This problem that you talked to me about," I began. "I can

see that it still exists."

"That's not what I came here to say."

"Shh," I said. "I can help, but only if you do exactly as I tell you."

He nodded.

"The girl," (I could not bear to say her name.) "The girl needs your help. You must go to her and take care of her. And you must not return here. I have nothing more that I can offer you. I have no further vision of your future."

"But..." He tried to hold onto my hand as I pulled it away.

"I've told you everything," I said, the room kaleidoscoped by my tears. "You have to go. Now." I said it loudly enough that my father rushed into the room. A policeman still, if not an employed one, he took the boy by the arm and led him out of the room. I ran to the kitchen, buried my sobs in the shelter of my Aunt Thessa's neck until I heard the distant latching of the downstairs door.

"Fate," my mother said, and clucked her tongue.

I didn't have the strength to tell her that what I had chosen was the opposite.

THAT night I lay on the green carpet, my eyes open wide and sleep impossible. All around me was the sound of my family breathing. Since the boy had gone, my mother and I had drifted around each other like ghosts, deathly and silent. Thessa and my father had huddled in the kitchen, talking too loudly and smoking cigarettes, Bento curled up on Thessa's lap as the television played The Price is Right and One Life to Live. By afternoon, the heat had grown oppressive; even with the windows open no air moved, but I breathed deeply, filled my lungs to bursting with euphoria. Later, those feelings of power disappeared. I had cheated the card by putting it on its feet. I had saved the girl from misery—perhaps. But I had also betrayed the one who had birthed me if not mothered me, the one who had taught me the living I was now choosing to abandon.

I closed my eyes, breathed as slowly and carefully as I could, trying to coax sleep from where it hid. The hiss of cars on the wet streets, the distant moan of trucks on the expressway just blocks away, did their work, but just as I began to sink into the gauzy darkness, I heard a sound so familiar that I had long ago ceased to notice it, but that now returned to me as if new—the soft scuff of my mother's slippers on the carpet, the uneven step, the barely audible sigh, as she ratcheted her bony hips, rolled forward on her fat Gypsy ankles toward where I lay.

The footsteps came closer, and I squeezed my eyes closed. I tried to slow my breathing, to make my rigid spine go lax. And then I heard her moan, the cracking of her ancient joints as she knelt and slowly lowered herself, until she lay on the carpet beside me.

"Mirena."

I squeezed my eyelids tighter. I tried to hold my breath. The hot, flowery scent of White Shoulders, which Aunt Thessa brought Mama from the counter at Filenes, perfumed the air around me. And when I did breathe, memories drifted into me, and I lived for a moment in the time before all of it had started, before the moon blood and the Advising and the demands and the rages, when Adriana Balnavera had been my Mama and I her little girl, all of those moments that would be forever lost. I felt her rough knuckles brush against my cheek.

"Daughter."

I opened my eyes. My mother's face hung over me like an eclipsed moon, the pockets of her cheeks, her coalblack eyes creped in shadow.

"You know, Mirena, I was once a young girl, too."

I reached up and pressed my fingertips to her mouth.

"No," I said. "You can't tell me what to do. Not any more."

What I expected then was tears or curses, indignation; I had lived with my mother long enough to know her swords and how she used them. But this time, only silence came. For a moment, we waited for what would happen next, two Gypsy women in the hour before dawn.

A sadness curled up with us on the carpet, and I imagined what it must be like to be a mother, to hold a baby in your arms and realize that one day you would be old, that the child would be grown and ready to take for herself all that you had enjoyed but could enjoy no longer, to avoid all the terrible mistakes you had made, to make a life that might be better than yours, not wasted and lost. And I knew then that my mother was afraid of me. With a word or a deed I could strike her dead.

"Come closer," she said. She rolled me toward her, and I put my cheek against her shoulder, nestled into the warm, milky space between her jawbone and the lobe of her ear. I lay my own ear against her chest, listened to the slow filling and emptying of her lungs.

"You know what I noticed," she said. "About that boy?"

Her thumb slowly stroked the back of mine. I closed my eyes, and her voice was like dreaming.

"I noticed the way he looked at you. For Christ, Mirena, he was terrified. Just like your father used to be."

"Still is," I said softly.

A low chuckle tumbled over in her throat, a sound I couldn't remember hearing ever, yet somehow it seemed a part of us, as if it had always been there.

In Among the Rushes

The crick ran high. It came down the valley in a flat, iron-red sheet, leaving the hedge of small willows on either side of it hip-deep in warm runoff.

Condell picked his way through the willows, ducking his tiny body through their branches, water sucking at his dungaree pockets, stooping to pull apart the clots of weeds that the slender branches sieved from the flood. He was not usually so careful, but that was the best way to find interesting things to keep—or give away.

The boy worried. The sun was already up above Hapman's silo, but he still hadn't found anything decent. A broken target arrow. A fishing plug with its paint half off. Nothing Lynette's baby would want.

He wondered if she'd had it yet. No. Mam would've hollered down from the house. Lynette must still be trying. The first one was the hardest. That's what all the women had been saying for months. And every time one of them said it, Lynette said she wasn't scared at all.

Condell wondered if she was still so brave. He looked back over his shoulder, through the willows and farther, up the yard to the house. They were inside, he knew. Mam and Pap and Lynette and Mrs. Hapman, waiting for the baby to come out.

Timmy Colebert wasn't there, Condell thought. He was the one Lynette got pregnant off of. Run off and joined the Army and left Lynette to have a baby on her own, and her only fourteen.

You never could tell what might happen if someone had a baby on their own. Orrin Kent's mam had him all alone, and she didn't care for him at all. Told him right to his face, pointing her cigarette at him while she talked, "You been nothin' but a weight on me, Orrin James Kent. Nothin' but a God-damn weight." Orrin acted like it hadn't bothered him at all, but Condell remembered. He didn't want Lynette to talk to her baby like that. He wanted things to get off to a good start.

Condell waded upstream. When he got as far as the big pool behind the tractor barn, he pushed through to the edge of the crick channel. A big willow bellied out at the head of the pool, its long, leafy whips dragging the water.

He pulled himself up onto the thick trunk. It was chilly in the shade, and Condell shivered as the water evaporated off his skinny legs. He watched the crick wash through the willow hedge, and remembered the stories Mam told him about Moses.

"The baby Moses was cast onto the waters on a raft," Mam said, "and the Lord held him up. He wasn't about to let him drown, sir. Moses was to be a holy man. They found him in among the rushes and raised him for their own."

Condell turned and watched the channel upstream, but nothing good came down. Dead branches. Chunks of yellow styrofoam. A plastic bread bag puffed up with air. Timmy Colebert promised Lynette he'd send her some of his Army pay, but none of it came, Condell thought. Mam and Pap had no money to buy the baby a present; Mr. Hapman didn't pay bonus till corn came in. All that Army pay and sendin' nothin'. How could Timmy be that way?

IT drifted into the pool just as he heard Mam's voice, calling out his name.

He could see her through the willows, standing down in bottom of the yard near the crickbed, her long, rusty hair flying, her hands cupped to her mouth. She wouldn't wait long before she came to hunt him. When Mam yelled, you best get to it.

She yelled his name again, this time louder, in a way that

meant she knew he was around but wasn't paying attention. But Condell didn't answer.

It was a ball that came floating down, the size of a sweet-melon and clear as glass. When the ball drifted closer, Condell could see more of its insides. There was a carousel, with painted horses, tiny jewels and mirrors.

"Con-dell! You get up to this house right now. And I mean it!"

The baby's here, Condell thought in one small part of his mind, but the rest was fixed on the ball. It was only feet away when he saw the children. There on the carousel, with new dress clothes and clean pink faces and smiles, like the children of the king he'd seen in a book one time. And they were alive. They were. They rode the horses, pulled on the leather reins, and Condell could hear them laughing as the circus music played.

The ball was closer, and Condell slid along the rough bark as far out over the crick as he could go. He stretched out his arms and the ball came toward him perfectly, as if the crick knew exactly where it was supposed to run. To hell with Timmy Colebert. He could keep his Army pay.

JUST before the ball slid past him, Condell saw the girl's face. She had long red curls and blue eyes, and sat, smiling and beautiful, on the back of a coal-black horse. She looked at him for a moment—he was sure of it—and when Condell came back to himself, the ball had slipped into the channel downstream of the pool.

He scraped down the trunk of the big willow as fast as he could and crashed into the hedge, rusty water splashing up into his eyes, branches smacking his arms and legs. He fell, then got up, and stumbled into the open field.

Mam turned around as she was almost back to the house and ran down through the yard to catch him. She latched her bony fingers into his hair for a hold, but he pivoted and tore himself away.

The bridge over to the main road was the last open spot before the crick got swallowed up by the willows again. Condell stood on it and watched as the ball slipped downstream, gone forever.

Mam caught him there on the bridge, but he dodged her again, this time running for the house. "God damn you, Condell Lewis," she hollered from behind, and he ran harder. His heart was hammering now, and his breath was coming quick; he churned up through the yard past the old tipped-over refrigerator and the pile of rotting chimney brick. He reached up, banged back the screen door and hoisted himself through the doorway into the near darkness inside.

THE room smelled like a new calf. Condell stood near the doorway and leaned against the wall, listening for the noise of a baby crying, hearing his own furious heartbeats and nothing more. His eyes got used to the dark, and he saw Lynette stretched out naked on a mattress on the floor, slick with sweat.

Mam came through the door with a scream clamped in her teeth; Condell could hear it trying to break out. Pap stood over Lynette with something covered up in a blanket. Condell could tell by the way Pap held it that what was in the bundle was a dead thing.

"Daddy, what was it?" Lynette said, swallowing air.

"Boy." Mam answered in her husband's silence, her voice coming out like it was pried. "Russell, take Condell out to the tractor barn. Make a box. Take it out there when you go, unless Lynette wants to hold it a minute."

Lynette didn't answer.

Mrs. Hapman sat at the kitchen table, a cigarette burning slowly in her bony hand.

CONDELL and Pap built the box together, Condell bracing the rough board across the wooden horse while his father sawed.

The screen door slammed, and Condell heard Mrs. Hapman say goodnight. Lynette's sobs started, then got louder as Pap hammered in the blunt roofing nails.

"Daddy," Condell said. He pointed at the box. "It ain't supposed to be square. Supposed to cut off the corners at an angle."

"Don't matter."

"People will see it at the funeral," Condell said. "Say her baby only had a half-made coffin."

"There won't be no funeral," Pap said.

"There will."

"Condell." Pap sat down on the footboard of the tractor. He wiped the sweat from his high forehead with the back of his hand.

"It wasn't ever alive. Ever. Didn't get a name. Wasn't baptized. It ain't really nobody, nobody at all. We can do our own service up on the side hill. Mr. Hapman'll read. Lynette will take it easier if her baby is close to the house. Understand?"

"Timmy Colebert is a son of a bitch," Condell said.

When the box was finished, Pap put the baby in it and nailed it closed. They carried it back to the house in the dark.

MAM sat at the kitchen table in a grey nightgown, drinking coffee from a scabbed enamel cup.

"Put it there on the floor," Mam said, pointing to a place near where Lynette lay sleeping on the mattress. "I think she wants to be close to it for a little bit. Even if she says she don't. Condell, you get to bed now. I laid out your good clothes."

"Mam," Condell said. "Will Lynette's baby go to heaven?"

Mam took a drink of her coffee. "It ain't time to talk about that," she said. "Give me a kiss and go to bed."

CONDELL'S room was at the back of the house, with a screened window that looked out onto the hayfield. The boy knelt on his bed with his arms resting on the window ledge, watching the lightning bugs flash. He waited until the house was completely quiet, then crept out to the living room.

The weight of the box surprised him. It was too heavy to be not anyone at all. He laid it on the floor near the door and went out first, then pulled it slowly across the sill, stopping to make sure Lynette was still asleep. He could hear the crick swishing down the valley, see the willow hedge nodding in the moon-light. He pressed the box against his chest and walked slowly across the yard.

It was black dark underneath the bridge. Condell rested the little coffin on the ledge of stones at the edge of the crick and waded in. The pool dropped off deep from a ledge just a foot or so in. Condell went under in the warm, black water and bobbed up, dogpaddled back to the ledge and pulled the box in with him.

"Moses," Condell said, and the word echoed off the bridge's steel girders.

The box dipped below the surface, but came back up and rode fine. Condell kicked slowly into the middle of the pool, pointed the box downstream and let it go. He backpedaled against the current and watched in silence until it disappeared.

Killing Houdini

For nearly sixty years since his last escape, Harry Houdini had been bound securely in the trunk of my past. I know magic, and had made my living by it. I had worked as best I could to make him vanish forever. And until Ms. Helena Stith-Davis intervened, I had maintained a carefully crafted illusion: the Great Houdini, as far as most of the world knew, had been killed anonymously. Mine was the unwatched hand, performing the trick of death without detection.

Ms. Stith-Davis first reached me on a Tuesday morning in early June. Spring comes late to Montreal, and pale, halfhearted sunlight drowsed into the front window as I puttered amongst the magicians' capes and wands, the golden coins and disappearing eggs and silk handkerchiefs. The window's thick, dusty glass magnified the heat, and it oozed invitingly into my cold and ancient bones. The telephone's ring, when it came, might have been a sound I imagined, rather than heard; it went on for some time, I would guess, before I responded.

"Merlin's Magic Supply. Quentin Strake speaking," I said, as I had uncountable times before. "How may I help you?"

The voice of Ms. Helena Stith-Davis, which I heard for the first time but not the last, conjured the image of the blunt, relentless woman that I had long ago grown to fear.

"Tell me exactly what you know about the death of Harry Houdini," she said in a tone that carried no detectable human emotion. "All of it. Leave nothing out."

Once more—perhaps, I hoped, for the final time—the trunk had been opened.

I had wanted to die without facing Houdini again, but might have known better; completely disappearing after killing the most famous con man the world had ever known would be a feat of legerdemain beyond the abilities of the Great Houdini himself.

Con man, you might wonder. Houdini? And if you do, then you understand as much of him as most have, who believe that his artistry consisted of a magician's honestly-won deception, when it instead was composed of base fraud. I have studied the man, and I will reveal the truth—or at least part of it. While reports of Houdini's strength and ability to endure pain are accurate, his skills as an escapist are not. His true talent was his ability to conceal a skeleton key, to secret on his person a tiny blade with which ropes could be severed, and cheap, easy freedom obtained. He could spot weakness in people as well as in padlocks, could parlay his charm and celebrity into collaboration, could prise from those who knew it the information he needed to figure out the intricacies of a purportedly "escape-proof" hasp lock or prison cell. In my opinion, there was little magic in that.

As I have mentioned, I have my own secrets, and over the years I have kept them well. Helena Stith-Davis was not the first inquisitor I had faced. Among the others were a Miss Eileen Darlansky from the Toronto Globe and Mail in 1957, brushed off with a curt refusal for interview. William James Butler from the Albany Courier in 1968, sent packing by my loyal landlady, Eleanor Buffin, who defended her homestead with such zeal that he never returned. And Ludmeel Stephenson of the McGill University Alumni Association—my particular favorite, if there can be said to be one—hoodwinked into believing that to reveal the truth would have launched repercussions as far-reaching as the United Nations. Yet this new inquiry, like the others, meant the risk of exposure. It was once again time to perform my magic.

I set down the phone for a moment, walked to the front of the shop and turned the sign about so that it read Closed to any passers by. I dimmed the lights. On the way back to the counter, I stopped to rearrange a cluttered stack of top hats. Once a reliable seller, they had been moving slowly, like everything in the shop. At the end of the twentieth century, science was pushing magic to the verge of irrelevance.

I had no sooner picked up the phone than Ms. HS-D was at me again.

"I'm coming to Montreal as soon as possible to interview you, Mr. Strake. At your age, time is important. I know you have the information I'm looking for. If you'll just confirm that, I'll book my flight."

Like many young people, she knew only the disadvantages of age, not the advantages. I parried with feigned confusion.

"Houdini? Dead?" I said, trying to sound as if my mouth were toothless and clotted with oatmeal. "But you'd have to expect that. I'm 92 years old myself. If Houdini were alive, he'd be well over 100. Tell me, are you selling something?"

It was then that Ms. Stith-Davis revealed the uncommon resistance to distraction that magicians both admire and despise.

"Mr. Strake, perhaps I should share a little bit about my project with you," she purred. (Purred. I mean that. I shudder even now.) "I am currently a writer in residence at Sabinch College in Pittsburgh, Pennsylvania. I'm working on a biography of Miss Cynthia Broadhurst Elbow. Of the Pittsburgh Elbows, with whom I am sure you're familiar. Miss Elbow's diary prominently features her relationship with a Quentin Strake. I believe you and he are one and the same."

At that moment, my options vanished. I was certain that I heard Ms. Stith-Davis suppress a snicker.

"Harry Houdini," I said, speaking clearly and forcefully. "was ill to begin with. Seriously so. But they never mention that. It's always been me to blame, and nothing more."

"Not exactly," she cooed. "No one has ever mentioned your name specifically, Mr. Strake—other than Miss Elbow, I mean."

"So you'll be the first," I said. "Congratulations. After all these years, you've discovered the man who killed Houdini. You'll make the front page of the New York Times, for a day, maybe two. Now, go do your writing. Because I've given you all the information you're going to get."

My bluff was followed by an expectant silence. Just as I had nearly assembled the will to hang up, Ms. Stith-Davis spoke again.

"That's a disappointment, Mr. Strake. But I'm not some tabloid reporter. I am a scholar. And I'd as soon keep your secret—in return for some information."

"About?"

"My research subject, Mr. Strake. Cynthia Broadhurst Elbow."

"Cissy Elbow," I shouted into the phone. "Is absolutely not up for discussion."

I smashed the phone down with such force that I snapped a piece from its cradle. But that was not the worst part. Ms. Stith-Davis, I knew, was as irresistible as the guillotine. I hastened home immediately to consult with my landlady, who shared my secret—or at least part of it—for as long as she had known me.

"CISSY Elbow?" Mrs. Buffin said, raising a coquettish smile. "That was her name? My Lord, Mr. Strake, but you do have a past."

It was the first time that I had told Mrs. Buffin—or anyone else—about Cissy, whom I had not seen since I fled to Ottawa after Houdini's death, and whose own death I had learned of through obituaries in the Montreal papers a dozen years before. It seemed unbelievable that so much time had passed, that I had kept Cynthia Elbow imprisoned in my mind for so many years, like a girl trapped forever in the disappearing trunk. But the plain fact was that I had forced Cissy into that box, and that with every glimpse of her that reappeared, I felt a freshened pain.

"Houdini," I said to Mrs. Buffin, trying to push Cissy away. "That's what that grave-robber really wants. I am sure of it. She knows I am the one who killed him, and is using what she knows about Miss Elbow to pry more information from me."

What information I had—or would surrender—was limited, yet it would be enough to make the career of a university biographer, if it could be told in my own words. Of that I had no doubt.

IF you have not heard of the circumstances of Harry Houdini's death—and, more importantly, if you have—let me tell you about them. I have been alloyed with Houdini, intimately though anonymously, for nearly seven decades. I know what the sources say. And I know the exact ways in which they differ from reality.

The Montreal Diarist explained it this way, as most newspapers have since: Houdini died after receiving a blow to the stomach from an admirer. The great escape artist often allowed fans to test his strength by punching his abdomen as hard as they could. This time, the admirer struck before Houdini could tense his abdominal muscles. The internal injuries proved fatal.

The sources seldom reveal that at the time of his death, Houdini suffered from acute appendicitis, a condition that might well have killed him regardless, given his suspicions of the medical profession and his belief in his own invincibility. The admirer is further identified only as "a student." There has never been mention of the student's name.

Some simple facts, then, to fill in the disappeared parts: I, Quentin Strake, killed Harry Houdini in the manner reported. After doing so, I fled to Ottawa, where I opened my first magic supply shop—indeed, hiding where I could be least expected, a feat worthy of any decent magician. I spent a decade in Ottawa, then returned to Montreal, where I opened Merlin's, another shop of the same type. I have lived at the fringe of Houdini's world—the world of magic—for nearly all of my life. Yet my exile to Ottawa, my subsequent efforts to maintain a low profile, seemed mostly unnecessary. Over the years, the world had mostly disappeared me, distracted by events important and not so. Until now.

"CYNTHIA Elbow," Ms. Helena Stith-Davis began, the moment I sat down at the table at Chez Henri. Her persistence had, after a week or more, worn me down. There were numerous phone calls, telegrams, even a substantial bouquet of flowers. Yet it was ultimately innuendo that brought me to agreement. She had hinted that Cissy's diary, or a copy of it, might be loaned me, if and only if I promised secrecy—an irony I did not fail to notice. I'd found this irresistible, although after agreeing to meet her, I began to despise my weakness almost immediately.

Ms. HS-D was considerably more attractive than her telephonic demeanor implied—thick, lustrous black hair, pale, flawless skin, eyes of deep green—yet the stern grey suit she wore, the severe way she arranged her coif, seemed designed to deflect attention rather than attract it. She withdrew a tiny tape recorder from a black leather handbag and switched it on, spoke the date clearly, naming me as "Quentin Strake, Interview Subject One Twenty-Seven." I silently pitied those who had come before.

"Tell me how you met her," she said.

"Cissy?"

Ms. Stith-Davis rolled her eyes.

"Not a topic for consideration," I said. "Next question."

"But the main topic of my project, Mr. Strake. Surely you must understand." She smiled insincerely, and I noted a mildly humanizing gap between her lower front teeth. I judged it a design flaw rather than an indicator of character.

I called the waiter and ordered two helpings of Scotch whiskey. I can hold my liquor; I hoped fervently that Ms. Helena Stith-Davis could not.

"Houdini first," I said, after we had indulged a few sips. Her eyes widened with interest. Direct denial had failed me, but the misdirection, a sleight central to all magic, did not. The technique was simple: focus the attention of the audience on a dazzling, yet unimportant object, while you conceal or manipulate the object of importance.

"I did not intend to kill him," I said, "That's the first thing I want you to believe."

For a moment, just as I began to tell it, my memories vanished. This is something I have gotten used to, something that no longer embarrasses me, or makes me feel useless and ended. It has become a condition of my life, my age, and nothing more. I waited a few seconds, then my mind fastened onto a brilliant piece of scarlet: the initials "H.H." embroidered on the lapel of Harry Houdini's immaculate black tailcoat. The memories were there again, alive and whole, like a dove fluttering from an illusionist's palm, or Houdini's long black tails flapping in the wind.

"It was on the campus at McGill, in autumn of 1926," I said to Ms. HS-D. "The afternoon before his evening performance at the Odeon. He was showboating, of course. Heaving barbells about. Slipping handcuffs and the like. The kind of preview he did before every show to ensure a packed house. Small illusions, really, compared to what he would later do. But they worked well enough."

I could see it now as if it were happening not seventy odd years ago, but at this very moment. A crowd of students gathered on the lawn near a dormitory. Houdini, the wind churning up from the river and rattling his tailcoat, ruffling his thick, dark hair. He swaggered, strode across the tiny wooden stage, rooted about in the adulation, his voice booming over the crowd. I wish I could say that I disliked him instantly. Yet part of the adulation was mine.

The opinion of Cynthia Broadhurst Elbow, who had come with me to see the preview, differed considerably from my own.

"He's repulsive, Quentin," she announced as the performance went on. "Look at him, will you. All muscle and no intelligence. He reminds me of one of Father's company men."

Cissy grasped my arm firmly, and began to tug me away. But then Houdini spotted her.

"Miss," he called. "Don't leave yet. We've just begun."

Cissy ignored him. She pulled harder at my arm.

Houdini called out again, louder this time, and the crowd turned its collective head. "Do I make you afraid, Miss?"

At the sound of the word afraid, Cissy Elbow stopped as if hypnotized and turned toward the stage. She met Houdini's gaze with all the resolution she could muster.

"You haven't the capacity to scare me," she said.

Houdini knew better than to bully. "Well, I believe that's probably true, Miss," he said warmly. "But come up, now. Please. Because I need someone of fortitude and daring to give me assistance."

If there were two words to describe Cissy Elbow, fortitude and daring would be they. She was hard as the steel from her father's mills, and her personality, like that steel, seemed forged from some great heat. In a time when women of her set were considered little more than ornaments, to be sent to the parlor or to the lounge decks of cruise steamers while the men discussed important matters, she drove sports cars, climbed mountains, shot a lion in the African bush. She aroused fear in men rather than feared them.

Still, the men in the crowd who stood closest to Cissy fixed her with unabashed stares. Cissy was beautiful; as much as it sometimes pained me, I could not deny it. The day we first saw Houdini, she kept her thick, rufous-blonde hair pulled back from her face with an emerald-silk scarf which brought out the depth of her coalsmoke eyes, the sharp rise of her cheekbone and the perfect scarlet slash of her lips. Her white blouse and martin-black skirt conformed perfectly to her shape, which was, quite contrary to the notion of beauty in 1926, defined in broad, lush curves. It constantly amazed me that such a woman would choose me for company, and every moment I spent without her I feared she had found the company of someone else.

"Would you give me the honor of presenting you on stage, Miss?" Houdini said. It was clear from the tone of his voice that though he wished he could patronize Cissy Elbow, he understood respect to be the only course.

"Victory," Cissy said, in a voice audible only to me. She gave my hand a squeeze, kissed me warmly and fully on the lips, and mounted the stage.

Houdini led Cissy up the steps of a wooden riser, until she stood above him, her feet level with his chest. He held out his hand, palm up, and invited her to step onto it. She showed no fear, so perhaps it was her intent to embarrass him. In any case, she refused to comply.

The illusionist climbed up the riser then, and stood next to Cissy, leaned toward her with his back to the audience and spoke quietly to her, so that none in the audience could hear. I marveled at the way he made all of us who watched, all of us whom he had been so aware of just moments before, seem to vanish for those few suspended moments.

Apparently, the performer's encouragement sufficed. He stepped down from the riser, looked up at Cissy, and gestured again. Her body trembled a bit, yet after a hesitation of only a second or two, she stepped from the platform onto his upturned palm.

The crowd gasped; it seemed impossible that he had the strength to hold her at all. Then total silence took over, as, with one hand, Houdini lifted Cissy above his head and carried her about the stage as a waiter would carry a tray. He held her there for several minutes, then slowly, gently, he lowered her to the earth, with no indication of strain. The crowd applauded madly. Houdini took a deep bow. Cissy, somewhat abashed, left the stage as soon as she could. The preview was over.

"Brute strength tempered only by self-love," Cynthia said, after debarking from the platform. "The worst possible combination for a man." But my admiration for Houdini continued to grow.

I had hoped this story, riven with spangles and celebrity, would be enough to distract Ms. Helena Stith-Davis. But she was a difficult audience, kept her eye on the hand she was not supposed to be watching, even while she enjoyed the show.

"Did Cissy ever tell you what Houdini said to her on that stage," Ms. HS-D inquired.

She had already finished her second Scotch, and seemed none the worse for wear. I took a sip of my own and noted that my hand was shaking.

"Miss Elbow never mentioned."

"Too bad. A brush with fame is always interesting. But not as interesting as the recollections of a most intimate companion, don't you think? So could we discuss some of those?" Ms. HS-D swallowed the rest of her drink, and to intimidate me, I am certain, called the waiter and ordered two more.

"I am tiring," I said, over the rim of my scotch, trying to sound so, which was not difficult at my age. I hoped that my feigned fatigue added to the air of disinterest I tried to project.

"I'm in need of a nap," I said, manufacturing a smile. "You'll understand it when you reach my age. But before I go, I 'd like to ask about the diary you mentioned. Cissy's diary. Have you brought a copy with you?

Ms. HD-D smiled coyly, but not without genuine sympathy, I thought. Her soft hand grazed my arm.

"Perhaps," she said. "I'll bring it when we meet again."

The interview was over.

"**SHE** thinks she can take advantage of me because I am old!" I shouted, startling Mrs. Buffin so that she nearly upset her tea.

I sat at her sturdy, oak-topped kitchen table, behind her tightly-drawn shades, and sipped a mug of Earl Grey, gamely nibbled the sandwich she made of her own crusty rye bread and thick slices of smoked gouda. The telephone in my apartment upstairs burred relentlessly. My nemesis Helena Stith-Davis was the cause of it all.

"She'll give up," Mrs. Buffin said, "Americans often do." A hopeful smile creased the soft lines of her face, and the fractured crystals of her blue eyes shimmered. I had not known Mrs. Buffin as a young woman, or even seen a picture of her then. But at 84, the shadows of beauty remained.

"Perhaps she will," I said, but I had little hope. It had been more than a week since the meeting at the restaurant. Business at Merlin's had continued at its customary slumberous pace, and I had been left to wander the aisles of my decrepit shop with little more than the probable content of Cissy Elbow's diary on my mind.

What could be the worst of it? That Cissy and I were lovers? We had been, of course, if even for the shortest time, but lovers in the old-fashioned sense—although there had been some physical aspect to it all. That I had killed Houdini? Ms. HS-D already knew this, and I had confirmed it. There was one more possibility that remained, and the question was this—had Cissy committed the facts to paper, or was I the only one who knew?

The phone stopped ringing for a generous minute. Then it began again. I set my teacup down and pushed my sandwich aside.

"If she gets what she wants," Mrs. Buffin said, "It won't be from me."

It was an unnecessary promise, both of us knew. A loyal illusionist's assistant, she had kept my secret for decades.

YOU might wonder why I would tell anyone, even someone as true as Mrs. Buffin, that I killed Harry Houdini? Relief, mainly. Can you imagine keeping a secret that not only haunted you, but would haunt the entire world, if only it were revealed? The newspapers seemed mostly to have forgotten Houdini, but there were thousands, maybe hundreds of thousands, of people who, more than half a century after his death, worshipped him, or should I say, the person they believed he had been. I pictured them out there, linked to me by invisible wires that crossed time and distance, and by the gruesome yet durable riddle I answered: Who killed Harry Houdini? The riddle was simple, yet containing its answer was agonizing.

Why Mrs. Buffin in particular? She was honest. Unperturbable. Prone to understanding the weight of circumstances in trying times. She was, in short, the most Canadian woman I have ever known. We Canadians have endured cold and shortened day-light. Invasion and conquest. Cultural warfare. The United States of America in all its beastly forms. But still, we have endured. We are slow to excitement. We listen before talking. We are reluctant to condemn. Eleanor Buffin exemplifies all these traits, and that is why I trusted her then, and still do. Yet even with Mrs. Buffin at my side, I feared what might happen next.

That night, having sneaked into my apartment by the back stairs after sundown, I lay alone in my room, the headlamps from the occasional passing automobile throwing wands of light around the edge of the drawn windowshades that arced across the ancient floral wallpaper and magicked my soul. For most of my life, I had been surrounded by what was commonly called magic, but in fact was merely illusion, the assemblage of deceits, sometimes simple, sometimes incredibly complex. For all those years, those decades I had performed a single illusion—that which was my life—the simplification of the death of Houdini, the careful elimination of certain incriminating facts related to the event, the misdirection of all who approached the event in search of the truth. Now, when I saw that all of those years had come down to nothing more than a single deceit, the waste of it overwhelmed me, and I wept. But even as the tears fell, I knew that I would do all that I could to see the illusion maintained.

WITH my landlady's support, I built a siege line against the relentless appeals of Ms. Helena Stith-Davis. I changed my telephone number to an unlisted one. I hung a sign in Merlin's Magic Shop that said simply "Out." I moved to and from my apartment only under the cape of darkness, and made Mrs. Buffin's apartment into my daytime safe house. The phone stopped ringing, and the silence was painful and sweet. But just as I convinced myself that my persecutor had surrendered, a large manila envelope arrived by post.

Addressed simply to Strake, 42 Rue de Hudson, and wrapped in plain brown paper, the package promised little. But the perfume with which the parcel was scented exploded along my spine like a burst of freed doves. It frightened me deeply that Ms. Stith Davis could have located a bottle of Chanteuse Bleu, Cissy Elbow's customary fragrance, as it had been out of production for more than half a century. But its warm, willowy scent conjured Cissy instantly. I could see her as clearly as if she stood before me, hear her effervescent laughter. It was as if an imprisoned receptor in my brain had suddenly struggled from its bonds.

But Chanteuse Bleu was the least of the resources to which the calculating Stith-Davis was privy. Inside the fragrant parcel was a photograph, or should I say, a poorly-executed photocopy of one, which proved my olfactory-charged memory unequal to the engineering genius of Mr. George Eastman, inventor of the Kodak. There before me was Cissy Elbow in the flesh.

My God. Cissy Elbow, after all those years. Cissy Elbow, who came from America with her smart clothes and her money. Cissy Elbow, who loved her father dearest of all men, and drove every other man wild. Cissy Elbow, who smoked cigarettes, drank straight vodka with a lime twist, drove a silver REO at speeds that defied light, and danced to Negro jazz before Canada knew it existed. Cissy Elbow, who called me darling when no other woman would consider me, chicken-limbed, sober Quentin Strake. Cissy Elbow, who let me kiss her unclothed breasts but go no further, and I did not want to go further, because that was enough.

In the photograph, she wore a battered Panama hat, her thick, tangled hair barely contained, a dam that might burst at any second. She wore a men's wool hunting suit, its loosely cut trousers defining her broad, soft hips, and she held a bamboo fly rod in her hand. In short, she looked stunning, which was something I had forgotten she could do in almost any cut or style of clothing. But it was her expression that nearly stilled my heart. Though the photocopy was scarcely legible in many respects, the whole living world of that place, that time, was captured in her eyes. Her smile, directed not at the photographer but the world at large, held back nothing, promised everything from a flirtation to a lifelong love affair, from hours of animal coupling to the perfect love of a mother for her child.

To understand the power of this photograph to arouse my soul, you must know that I loved Cissy Elbow deeply—even if she did not return my affection to the same degree. Did she love me? I believe she did—yet incompletely. Did she refuse me when I finally gathered the courage and asked her to marry me? Immediately, but with such kindness that even the pain of her refusal, which would never leave me, was somewhat assuaged. Yet still, nearly seventy years later and her long in the grave, she held my heart prisoner.

I turned the photocopy over; on the back, Ms Helena Stith-Davis had written a note:

If you think she looks beautiful here, you should see the original print. In fact, you should own it. And that is, in theory, possible. I have the negatives for this—and six more. Another chat? 225.3285. Helena.

That night, I scarcely slept. My mind was a roaring tide, crashing repeatedly against a single great stone: What was Cissy Elbow worth to me? Memories were all I had of her, and those were slowly vanishing from my mind. From the thin air had appeared a chance to have her, finally—or as much as I could hope to have in this lifetime. To conjure her from the very dead. The photographs. The Chanteuse Bleu. Yet to get them, I would have to give up something of great value, which I had possessed for most of my life.

"ROMANCE," Mrs. Buffin said, peering intently over her tea-cup, a girlish smile rising quite unexpectedly to her face. "That's all they seem to be interested in these days. That's what this Ms. Davis wants to know about, sure enough. Your relationship with Miss Elbow—" Blushing, she tuned away.

"It's all right," I said. "Go on."

"Go on, yourself," Mrs. Buffin said. "Tell that writer the truth. She will either copy it in her book—or write a lie. You'll be done with her then, and she with you."

My landlady sounded so certain of herself that for a moment she nearly convinced me. But then reality swept before me like a wand, transforming the illusions of hope to cold, bare, reality.

"Eleanor, I—"

She turned toward me then, with a look of surprise that startled me.

"Eleanor?" she said quietly. Not once in our twenty-seven year relationship had I used her given name.

"Excuse me," I said, feeling my face redden. "I am under strain, Mrs. Buffin, and—"

"Eleanor, please."

"Eleanor," I said, and I felt my heart shaking. "I have told you the truth, but only part of it. And Ms. Stith-Davis will not be satisfied until she has heard everything."

"If you wish to unburden yourself, Quentin," Mrs. Buffin said quietly, pulling her chair next to mine and taking my hand in her own. Her expression showed that no matter what I admitted to, she was ready to forgive me. The sheer beauty of this notion nearly raised me to tears, but still, I could not confess. If I were to do so—God forbid—it would be to Ms. Helena Stith-Davis, whom I had reluctantly agreed to meet that very afternoon.

"MR. Strake, it's so nice to see you."

Ms. Helena Stith-Davis gingerly held out her hand, presented this greeting without a trace of the irony that drilled me to the core.

We met this time at the Colfax Luncheonette, a place that seemed more suitable for the unseemly interaction that was about to take place. I slid into the booth without comment, remembering Mrs. Eleanor Buffin's words of advice about simply telling the truth. Yet I did not feel inclined to do so.

"I have decided to be brief and to the point," Ms. HS-D said, pulling a large manila envelope from her dusky leather briefcase as she spoke. She lifted its flap briefly so I could see the sheaf of glossy black and white photographs inside. "I have something you want, Mr. Strake. And you have something I want. The decision is yours."

I had made up my mind beforehand. I took a deep breath and began.

True enough, I told Ms. HS-D, I went to Houdini's room, later in the evening of his McGill performance.

The reason for my visit was simple. The more I considered the way not only his physical strength but the power of his personality had affected the audience, the more I admired him. I did not yet know his true nature, and I believed him to be everything I was not—strong and fearless, bold and dashing, a man of uncommon power. I wanted to change myself, to learn his secrets and become the man I was not for one and only one reason—to make Cynthia Broadhurst Elbow love me completely.

HOUDINI stayed that night at the Imperial Hotel, a magnificent palace of a building located just off the campus on Rue de Stanley. Using the application of what little cash I could muster, I obtained the illusionist's suite number from a bellhop. While others attended Houdini's show that evening, I spent the time gathering my courage, with the help of some Scotch and a dozen cigarettes. Still, when the time came, I nearly surrendered to fear. Then I thought of the pleasure of kissing Cissy's breasts, and how that pleasure might be mine forever. It was half past eleven when I left my apartment, on course for events that would change my life in ways I could not imagine.

Nervous as a schoolboy, I dodged the desk clerk in the Imperial's lobby, slipped up the stairwell to the east wing and made my way to Houdini's top-floor suite. I can still recall the hum of the lighting, smell the stale odor of carpet too long from the air, mixed with the scent of cigars. Three doors down from number 1219, I suffered a last minute attack of doubt, but closed my eyes and thought of Cissy until it vanished.

When I knocked, the door eased open a crack, until it met the end of the chain that secured it. A small, stout man with sharp brown eyes peered suspiciously through the gap.

"You have no business here," he said. "Go away or I will call the police."

No sooner had the man spoken than Houdini himself had moved him aside, slid the chain open with professional ease.

"Mr. Melnick here is a bit out of sorts," Houdini said, smiling and beckoning me inward. Do come in, Mr..."

"Carleton," I lied, not knowing why I did.

We were at the borders of infamy then, all of us in the room. Introductions were exchanged, and I began to try to express the reason for my visit. Yet suddenly, it seemed ridiculous. How could a total stranger, in a moment or two, teach me how to win the heart of the woman I loved? The foolishness of my mission seemed utterly clear. I abandoned it and fell back on the only alternative I could bring to mind.

"I have heard that your stomach is as rigid as steel," I said. "May I strike you there?"

As odd a request as it seemed to me then, Houdini had heard it hundreds of times before. He nodded his assent, then turned to speak to Mr. Melnick. It was then that I struck.

It was not the force of the blow, but its timing, which made it lethal. Houdini had not yet tensed his muscles, and the punch took him by surprise. I, too, was shocked—to feel my hand meet not a wall of hardened muscle, but to proceed onward, deep into a pocket of soft flesh and tissue. Houdini released the tiniest, least audible expression of pain. Instantly, his face drained of color.

"I must ask that you leave, sir," the escape artist said politely, as soon as he had recovered his voice. What he did not know was that his appendix was inflamed, and that the blow I struck ruptured it. Twelve hours later, on a train trip to Detroit, the world's greatest escape artist, the man whom no chains could bind, would be bound forever by the chains of death. And I was bound to him, though in anonymity, forever.

WHEN I had finished the telling, Ms. Helena Stith-Davis paused in silence for a moment, dragged her spoon several times through her untouched cup of coffee.

"You are leaving something out," she said. "I cannot prove this, and you know it. But now you must tell me, Mr. Strake, if you are to get what you want." Her voice had lost all pretense of warmth. She slid the packet of photographs toward me, yet kept it under the protective cover of her palm.

I was 92 years old, and had maintained the illusion for nearly seventy years—longer than even Houdini could. What Ms. Helena Stith-Davis suspected, she could never prove. And I had no doubts that despite the angry look she focused across the table, the photographs would be mine no matter how I answered. One more misdirection, one more lie, and I could take the illusion to the grave. Yet I could not bear it.

"Before I tell the truth," I said. "I must be certain that the photographs will be mine."

Ms. H S-D hesitated only a second before sliding them across the table. I opened the envelope and tilted out the sheaf of photos, gazed for a moment at Cissy's face, and then I gave my interrogator what she wanted.

My story had been complete and accurate until that fraction of a moment in which Houdini assented to my request and turned to talk with his assistant. At that moment, I glanced into a small mirror that hung on the wall outside the illusionist's sleeping quarters. In its reflection, I saw a woman, reclining on the bed. At first, I did not recognize her—or I would not—but then the scent of Chanteuse Bleu reached the back of my throat, and I knew.

How easily the demarcation between intention and outcome shifts. What had been a benign experiment—to test Houdini's engineering, as it were—became an exercise in the blackest hate. I hit him quickly—when I knew he was not prepared—and with all my might.

"My," Houdini said. "Oh, my," and he sat down on the sofa.

"And Cissy," Ms. HS-D asked.

For the first time, I heard emotion in her voice, an interest that was based not on her quest for information, but on her compassion toward another human being.

I could have tried to describe to Ms. HS-D what I saw that day, yet I did not. Cissy rushed to the doorway, leaned against it, wrapped hastily in a pure white linen sheet, a goddess who had come to Earth to observe the brutal workings of men. The look of sadness on her face was absolute, and I knew at that moment that no matter what I could say or do, the ties between us had vanished forever.

"The door to the bedroom swung closed and she disappeared," I told Ms. HS-D. "I never saw Cissy Elbow again."

FOR all of my adult life, I had been part of a gigantic misdirection—that the killing of Houdini was a glorious accident. Only Cissy Elbow could have known the truth of it, and in a final act of grace, she had kept my secret. Yet now it was secret no more. I had arrived at the meeting with Ms. Helena Stith-Davis the simple answer to a riddle. Now, with the pictures of Cissy tucked under my arm, I left the meeting a criminal. The misdirection had ceased; what would come of it I could not tell.

I stepped from the entrance of the luncheonette into the mid-day sunlight.

"Murderer," I said quietly to myself, yet I felt no revulsion, no chill. Houdini had taken from me all my hope for a glorious life, and had destined me to the merely tolerable. Still, he had also taught me the skill that had allowed me to keep my crime a secret for so many years. Now, only one secret remained, and it would never be revealed.

What had Houdini said to Cissy Elbow on that stage, when all of us in the crowd thought he was whispering encouragement into her ear, chasing her fears away? An invitation to seduction? A promise of love? Whatever else, it was a flawless misdirection.

THE warm sun of spring at my back, I took the long walk homeward at a slower pace than usual, pondering the mysteries of it all. I returned to my apartment, secreted the photographs of Cynthia Broadhurst Elbow in the bottom of a desk drawer, locked the apartment securely, and made my way downstairs, where I rapped softly on the door of my landlady. She answered the door wearing a housedress and apron, a dusting of flour covering her hands. The smile she gave me showed that my arrival was not altogether surprising.

"Eleanor," I said, and once again my heart registered a fear I tried not to reveal. "I am not the man you think I am."

"I never imagined so," she said. "Come in. There's bread in the oven and the kettle's just hot."

Benefits

Except for the scaly yellow feet, which were molded from some kind of hard rubber and a true chore to walk in, there wasn't much about the chicken outfit that Royce hadn't already imagined. It was bulky, and bound to be hotter than a roofer's ass out on the ball field. Of course, the eyeholes weren't sufficient. They gave you no peripheral, and the view through their black mesh was swimmy and strange, like being pinned on some good hash, but without the benefit of the buzz.

Closing one of his own eyes, Royce peered out through the costume's eyeholes and regarded himself in the cracked Budweiser mirror, feathers and all. Fuck, he thought, Bubba the Blue Hen. How in hell did you end up here?

Lorraine Dewley was the answer to that question, same as she had been since the day they'd met at Brampton High in '98. Royce and 'Rainey'd been a couple since then, sometimes off but mostly on—up until a month before, when she'd headed out the door to her VW Rabbit with her daddy's old Army duffel under one arm and Mr. Britches the shih-tzu under the other. No question of shared custody there—she'd brought Britches home just after they'd found the place, a bitty nest above Wilson's Welding, rented cheap on Royce's promise to paint the place, exterior, at his earliest convenience. Which two years later, he still meant to get to, but Rainey'd ragged him about even to the end.

"While I'm gone," she'd said, tugging her ponytail through the back end of her new Blue Hens baseball cap, "which will be forever or until you get your shit straight—and that's pretty much the same thing as far as I can tell—why don't you finish that god damn paint job?" She'd hucked the duffel into the back seat and set Mr. Britches in the front passenger bucket, jumped in and slammed the door, and trundled out of the muddy parking lot toward her parents' house in Glen Lake, where she'd been holed up ever since. The separation broke Royce's heart, but something else broke it worse. She was seein' that fuckin' shortstop, and he knew it.

It was five in the afternoon, but still well above 80, hot for early June. Just standing in front of the mirror, Royce began to sweat, so he lifted off the blue hen's fiberglass cowl, being careful that the lip of the headhole didn't catch on his flappy ears. Without the cowl, he looked damned near handsome, a human-hen cross with a suntanned face, a good strong jaw, a rugged, twice-busted nose, and blue eyes certain ladies thought the world of. Trying to cheer himself up, he popped the smile that had drawn not a little pussy in his day, but the smile wouldn't stick. Rainey'd made it clear what she wanted, and had made it clear for months.

"Full medical benefits, Royce. That's what I'm talking here. And if you don't find a job that has 'em, I will walk out this door, and you will be very, very sorry." He hadn't. She had. And he was.

It seemed ass-backwards that the benefits thing had been the bone they chewed on, when the real problem in Royce's opinion was why she wanted them—so they could have a baby.

"Hell, Rain," he'd told her the afternoon she first brought it up. They were fishing for smallmouth on Boone Pond in Royce's 12-foot johnboat. "Look at all we got here. The time to get out and do what we want, when we want. It doesn't get any better."

To Royce's surprise, Rainey'd let the baby idea go—at least temporarily. But after a month or two, the notion came back, and this time she held on. That's where the benefits came in. Her job at Thelma's Little Dickens Day Care didn't offer any, and that left things up to him. That was damned unfair, as far as Royce was concerned, but Rainey didn't see it that way.

"You got more options," she said during one particularly memorable go-round. "They won't hire a woman over at the cement plant. But you could get in, and you know it, Royce. People around here owe you."

"Owe me for what?" he said. But Royce knew. It was sports, all of them in general, but particularly baseball. On the mound at Brampton High, he'd chalked up 44 wins, including eight shut-outs and a state championship. He'd gotten a full ride to Paloma U., where, after a season of mediocre pitching and high-caliber drug abuse, he'd been shitcanned. But the folks in Brampton forgave and forgot. He was a local hero, after all. A job at the plant would be his for the asking, if he stepped back into the fold.

As far as Royce was concerned, none of it should have happened. He'd discovered when he was nine that he could throw a baseball harder than anyone he knew. It was a curiosity, and just that. But then his dipshit father had found out, and it was nothing but the sportin' life from there on in. Little League, then Babe Ruth. Baseball camp with Brad Stedworth, a second-rate major leaguer who'd molested half a dozen of the campers but taught Royce a great split-finger fastball. And high school stardom, which aside from the blowjobs was highly overrated. Nobody ever wanted to talk about anything with Royce Perry but baseball, and everybody wanted a piece of his so-called glory. Getting a job at the plant meant more than just nine to five and the hell that went with it. It meant starting the Royce Perry, All-Star thing over. And that was something he just couldn't do, even to stop Rainey from walking.

Besides, the plain fact was that her being gone wasn't exactly a tragedy—at least at first. She'd quit him before, but never for long. Royce figured he'd enjoy his freedom and wait her out. But then fate, in the form of Stephen J. VanSkyver, a light-hitting shortstop with good teeth, a fat wallet, and prospects for the future at his father's car dealership, had intervened. According to Billy Johnston, who wasn't entirely unreliable, Rainey and the shortstop had met at a charity auction, and of late, had been getting quite cozy, or as Billy put it, "They're past the friendly fucking stage, Royce. It's time you took some action." Those words put a scare in Royce. The girl wanted benefits, fine. He'd figure out some way. And he'd worry about the baby part later.

It was around that time that Royce heard about the mascot job with the Blue Hens, Brampton's minor league baseball club—and Stephen J. VanSkyver's current employer. Bruford Allen, Royce's old high-school football coach, managed the team, so landing the job was a piece of cake. The pay sucked wind, but it wasn't full time. And best of all, Bubba the Blue Hen, and his family or equivalent therof, received additional compensation, in the form of full medical benefits.

TURNING away from the mirror, Royce set the hen's cowl on the bed and shucked off his indigo wings. He tossed them on a laundry pile and strolled out to the kitchenette, dragging a dirty T-shirt and a pair of boxers along, snagged on his rubber feet. Pulling a chair out enough to accommodate his feathered jumpsuit, he slid in to the kitchen table, rummaged an ashtray for a decent-sized roach, sparked it on a handy Bic, put the phone receiver to his ear, and dialed. It picked up after two rings.

"Hello," he said. "Mrs. Dewley?," and turned his head to exhale. A cloud of dope smoke mushroomed toward the grease-enameled ceiling.

She couldn't wait to tell him about Rainey's new beau.

"Yes Ma'am," Royce said. "I heard a rumor about Mr. VanSkyver. A shortstop and the son of a millionaire. Quite a package. But I got some news for Lorraine, if she'd see fit to come to the phone."

Rainey wasn't home, or so her mother claimed. Janet Dewley had never been disposed toward treating Royce with kindness; as far as he was concerned, her word meant jack shit.

"Well, Mrs. Dewley," Royce said. "Could you take a message for me then? Tell Lorraine I got a new job."

Mrs. Dewley, as he'd forseen, was not impressed. But the message wasn't for her; it was for Rainey. He pushed ahead.

"It's a great opportunity," Royce said. "I'll still have access to the welding shop, so I can pick up some cash on the side. But this new job is a bit higher on the hog. Steady pay, and a solid benefits package. I wanted to share the details with Lorraine myself. But I can tell you that it's in marketing, and it's real high profile. You can pass that much along."

Mrs. Dewley promised she would, but now she had a question.

"The money I owe you and Mr. Dewley?" Royce answered. "Yes, Ma'am. I intend to start paying that back as soon as I get my first check. Just pass my message on to Lorraine. And give my fondest to your better half, won't you?"

With that, Royce dropped the phone on its cradle, took one last hit of the roach, dabbed it out with a spitwet finger, and tossed it down his throat. He wandered back to the bedroom, grabbed Bubba's blue wings and cowl, and headed for the car.

TEN minutes later, Royce eased his rust-scabbed Tercel into the parking lot of Blue Hen Field, a sheetmetal-roofed stand of bleachers and an announcer's booth that sat alongside the Cooper River on the outskirts of Brampton. Despite the Hens' traditionally weak position in the Atlantic Coast League, management kept the place up. The billboards had been freshly painted, the gaps in the chainlink outfield fence recently repaired. Royce shut down the engine, killed the last of a half-warm Bud, and slid out of the passenger seat. He fished Bubba's wings out of the hatch, untied the cowl from the roof rack, and carried them to the bleachers, where Donnie Lyaski waited in the afternoon sun.

"Hey there, Royce," Donnie said, running his stubby fingers through his graying whiffle-cut. His pale, mooney eyes loomed from behind enormous, thicked-lensed wire rims, secured behind his ears with a black elastic strap. A good-natured Pole from West Brampton, he'd suited up as Bubba the Blue Hen for the past seven years, through regular Coast League play from June to mid-August and in dozens of public appearances during the off season. But a few months back, he'd been cornered by a group of drunken Saco Sailors' fans at the opening of a car dealership, and, as he told the Brampton Examiner, "subjected to certain indignities" that he did not wish to discuss. Although the news would be kept secret to avoid adverse publicity, Donny'd had it. His Bubba days were over.

"Howdy, Big D," Royce said. He sat down on the first row of the bleachers and lit up a butt. "I guess you're here to give me the lowdown. That's damn decent of you. But it doesn't seem to me that there's a whole lot to it."

Donnie turned and looked wistfully toward the announcer's tower, as if envisioning an unavoidably tragic future.

"I wish you hadn't said that, Royce. You can't go in with an attitude. To people around here, Bubba isn't just a costume. He's a goddam franchise. There's honor at stake here, Royce. Brampton pride."

Donnie turned then, looked Royce straight in the eye. "To be honest with you, Royce, I tried to talk B.A. out of giving you the job. I'm not sure you're cut out for it." Behind his lenses, Donnie blinked.

"Ow," Royce said. "That god damn hurt. You been gettin' your lines from Rainey Dewley?"

Once again, Donnie looked away. "I'm definitely not gettin' into that, Royce."

"No, serious. Cause you sound like her."

"The thing about Bubba is…"

"Fuck Bubba. You think I can't do this? Watch me."

Royce stood up and started across the infield at a trot. Halfway to the pitcher's mound, he popped a round off, then fishtailed into a double handspring. He cartwheeled back to the bleachers, walked up them on his hands, and eased himself gently back onto his feet, his Marlboro still tucked in the corner of his lips. Panting a bit, he looked down at Donnie.

"Did Bubba ever do that with you under the hood? Did he?"

Donnie shrugged.

"You're damn right he didn't. Now I am going to put this costume on, and you are gonna teach me the basics. Rules and regs of bein' Bubba, so to speak. Nothing less and nothing more. And save the sermon for somebody else."

Royce suited up, and Donnie showed him all the routines. The Strut. The Chicken Scratch. The Wing Ding and the Bubba Bop. Royce caught on quick, adding some sauce of his own—a little sashay at the end of the Strut. A high kick that put a cap on the Chicken Scratch. A cartwheel and somersault into the Wing Ding. When practice was over, Royce jogged back to the Tercel and dug two more cans of Bud out from under the seat—one for him and one for Donnie. The sun had begun to fall, illuminating the hand-painted billboards on the right field fence with a glow that was almost heavenly. They sat on the bleachers for a while without talking, enjoying the beer and the cool breeze that whispered up from the river.

Finally, Donnie broke the silence. "Christ," he said. "You're gonna be a better Bubba than I ever was."

"Now Donnie, you know that's not true."

Behind his lenses, Donnie's eyes grew damp. "It is, Royce. I had the Bubba spirit, and that got me somewhere. But I'm no athlete. And you, well, you're a legend."

Royce had spent a good part of his life avoiding the truth,

and the pain that came with it. Lying came as easy as opening his mouth.

"Hell, D.," he said, giving Donnie a friendly clap on the shoulder. "I might spruce Bubba up a bit this year. But you made him. I mean, who invented the Strut? Who brought the Chicken Scratch to Brampton? And what about the time you flew off the visitors' dugout with two outs to go in that game against Portsmouth?"

"I fell, Royce."

"Flew, fell, who gives a fuck? I was there, D. I never seen a crowd crank up like that."

A smile found its way to Donnie's lips.

"I'm am here to tell you, D. that long after Royce Perry is dead and gone, they'll still be talking about Bubba the Blue Hen. And when they do, Donnie Lyaski will be the name they remember."

Donnie's smile got bigger. He took another swallow of beer. "Jesus," he said. "I never met anybody that could bullshit as good as you. But I appreciate it all the same."

He stood up and thoughtfully stroked his whiffle for a moment.

"Oh, Royce? One more thing. Watch out for the toddlers. They're the worst. A good ten percent of 'em will pee on you as soon as you pick 'em up. I figure it's the excitement. But it sure is a pain in the ass. I tried everything. Scotchgard, you name it. But not a one of 'em repels pee-pee."

"Thanks for the warning, Donnie."

"And Royce. I hope you get Rainey back. It's not the same around here without you guys together."

"Don't you worry about that, D," Royce said. "It's all part of the plan."

The whole way home, Royce grinned like a fox in the hen-house. Step one was accomplished. A job with benefits. Now it was time for step two—getting Stephen J. VanSkyver out of

Rainey Dewley's pants. He didn't quite have a plan for that—it was more like a scheme—but as far as he could see there wasn't a reason it shouldn't work. And that meant a reason to celebrate. On the way home he stopped and bought a fat sirloin, a pint of Jim Beam, and a cold six pack of Bud.

Royce opened the whiskey in the car, and by the time he got home, he was already buzzing. Dinner was one long, cozy blur—he woke up at nine that night with his cheek pressed in a sticky puddle on the kitchen table, the Jim Beam bottle empty and the phone receiver against his ear. He must've dialed it, but he had no recollection of that.

"Royce?" Rainey's voice echoed from the other end of the line. "Is that you?"

It took him a moment to unglue his tongue from the roof of his mouth.

"Did your mom tell you the news?" he said.

"What, that you're drunk again? Hardly news, Royce."

Of course she hadn't told Rainey, that bitch. For Christ's sake, wasn't there such a thing as common courtesy? But that wasn't important now. He needed to tell Rainey all of it, to let her know about the job, the full medical, and that he'd done it for her. But when he opened his mouth again, different words came out.

"Hey," he said. "What's the deal with you and that shortstop?"

"For Lord's sake, Royce," Rainey said, and hung up the phone.

THE Blue Hens' home opener fell on the second Saturday in June. And even though he hadn't thrown an overhand pitch in five years or better, Royce felt the familiar tingle he'd always enjoyed before the start of a game. Part of it was sheer nervousness over his—and Bubba's—premier, but a fair amount of chemical preparation had rubbed the burrs off that. Most of the jitter at his nerve endings was one of elation. The fucking catbird seat, that's what it was. The place where he'd put an end to Rainey and that shortstop once and for all.

From the window of his dressing room, a low-end RV provided by Karl Krane's Kountry Kampers and parked along the first base line, Royce watched as Hens' fans streamed in from the parking lot, toting styrofoam coolers and portable seat cushions, lugging babies like sacks of potatoes and dragging recalcitrant toddlers by their tiny arms. There was, he noticed purely as a matter of record, a shocking amount of tasty young tail among those in attendance, airing their freshly-hatched titties for the benefit of the crowd. For a moment he wondered if there might be some advantages to the single life he hadn't considered. But then he noticed Rainey, who'd slipped in under his radar and taken a seat in the front row, halfway down the third base line.

"Concentrate, asshole," he whispered to himself. This was no time for distractions.

With just a few moments before show time, Royce made some final adjustments to his wardrobe, smoothing down his breast feathers and making sure the rubber feet were laced tightly enough to prevent potentially hazardous slippage. That done, he picked up the walkie-talkie that lay on the vanity in the mobile-home bathroom and pressed the button that cued Irv Cate, the Hens' long-running public address announcer. "Hey Irv," Royce said. "I'm about set out here. Cue the theme when you're ready." He set down the talkie, took a deep breath, and headed for the RV door.

During his Bubba training session, Donnie hadn't give Royce a whole lot of advice. But one thing Royce remembered. "There's only one message," Donnie'd told him, "and that's showing the crowd you care."

As strains of "Dixie Chicken" drifted over the ballpark, Royce leapt down the RV steps, sambaed onto the field, stopped at home plate, and dipped into a low, courtly bow. He rose into a backflip, did a little soft shoe left, dropped to one knee, and spread his blue wings wide. The bleachers exploded. Fuck, Royce thought, this is going to be a piece of cake.

When the crowd had quieted down a bit, Irv Cate opened up the PA mike and cleared his throat, a sound not unlike that of a flushing urinal, yet deeper and with a more glottal timbre. The crowd grew silent in respectful anticipation. Then the silence burst.

"And now!" Irv roared through the loudspeaker, "It's time to introduce the starting lineup for your own BRAMPTON! BLUE! HENS!"

"Batting first, playing second base, number four, Joe Ciampi."

One by one, the Hens trotted onto the field. And as they did, Royce pumped the crowd to a frenzy. He clapped the second baseman on the back with his big blue wings, danced a jig with the center fielder. He let the catcher bowl him ass over tailfeathers, tucked into a roll and bounced to his feet. He strolled to the mound with the starting pitcher, fanning him with his wings. Then came the moment Royce had been waiting for.

"And finally, batting ninth and playing shortstop, Stephen J. VanSkyver!"

When Royce was hired, Bruford Allen had made one thing crystal clear. "Fuck up in public," B.A. had said, "or embarrass this organization in any way, and you are done. And don't think I'm pickin' on you cause you lost that game against Hudson your junior year. I've forgiven you for that fiasco. The rules go for everybody, not just you."

In light of this pronouncement, Royce had developed a simple strategy—to push the shortstop over the edge, and get him fired. He'd likely go back where he came from, Connecticut or some other godawful suburban shithole, and Royce would have Rainey to himself.

When the announcer called his name, Stephen J. VanSkyver

rocketed from the dugout at full bore, and Royce saw his every nightmare confirmed. The shortstop stood six-two, and weighed 225 if a pound. His biceps, perfectly tanned, were bulked up into leviathan slabs, and his uniform pants clung like paint to his powerful thighs. Blond curls tumbled out the back of his Hens' cap, and his stony jaw wore a day's worth of manly stubble. His smile was a wonder of modern orthodontia, and his blue eyes fairly glowed. In short, the cocksucker deserved to die.

But now, Royce realized, was not the moment to let hatred jam the gears. It was time to launch Plan A. As the shortstop grew closer, Royce spread his wings, a gesture that even had he wanted to, VanSkyver couldn't ignore. He dove into Bubba's embrace, and Royce pulled him close. A light scent of shaving soap wafted in through the Blue Hen's eyeholes.

"I had your mother up the ass," Royce shouted, as loudly as he could. "Repeatedly." And then he flung open his wings, sending Stephen J. VanSkyver jogging toward short, his stride hitching just a moment as he digested what he'd heard, or, possibly, what he was sure he couldn't have heard. Mission accomplished, Royce tore across the field, feathers rattling in the breeze, and headed to the stands, where he'd get the chance to do something he hadn't been able to do in more than two weeks, since the county sheriff pried him off the doorhandle of her VW at the Granite Oaks Shopping Centre—talk to Rainey in person. At least that was the idea, but as soon as he left the ball field, the toddlers attacked.

"Birdee!!!" one screeched, and they swarmed him like pigeons on a pile of corn. They tore off feathers and raked at his shins, stuffed magic markers through his beak hole and screeched for autographs, though he was certain not a one of them was old enough to read. The first time one peed on him, he nearly puked, but the second time, he didn't flinch—it was just kid pee, which most everyone knew was pretty much harmless, and it dried fast in the sun.

It only took Royce an inning or so to work his way through his fan base, but it wasn't until near the end of the game that he got the courage to approach Rainey. Of course, nobody in the stands would suspect his intentions. Bubba was known to be partial to ladies, and rumor had it that Donnie Lyaski had been a master at copping feels on the sly using Bubba as his front. For all anybody knew, Donnie and Bubba remained one and the same. Still, meeting Rainey in the stands was at odds with all his instincts—he'd had his share of public arguments, and in his experience, they always made the guy look bad. So he kept an eye open for his chance, and when Rainey headed for the refreshment stand in the top half of the sixth, he trailed her, his heart pounding and his palms wet as a sponge. Just as he had hoped, the stand was near deserted. He sidled up to Rainey and bumped her with his feathered shoulder like a bashful kid on a playground.

"Hi, Bubba, you big old hen," Rainey said, turning toward him and opening her lips into a halfsweet smile.

It wasn't the smile that killed him; it was the things about her that he'd already forgotten. The half-Southern drawl in her voice—a gift from her Father, an attorney who'd come to Brampton from Georgia in the seventies. The way she looked in a baseball cap, plain pretty with her straight red bangs and a spray of freckles across her nose. The worst of it was the smell of her, a soft, warm blend of Salem Lights and bubblegum that wafted in through Bubba's eyeholes and fairly poleaxed him. He counted to ten, reached out a trembling blue wing, and tucked her under it.

"Donnie," she said. "Don't you try anything funny."

Royce held on, not daring to move a feather. Even through the costume, he felt the contours of her hips, the warmth of her. His own body hummed.

"So," Rainey said. "You seen that asshole ex-boyfriend of

mine? I heard he bagged himself a slut the other night at the Cork and Bottle."

"That's a damn lie, Rainey. Who told you that?"

She wiggled out from under his wing.

"Royce?"

What he expected now was one of two things—a pitch-all tantrum or a complete surrender, but he didn't get either. Through the eyeholes, he saw Rainey cover her mouth. A giggle leaked out first, and then a bark of laughter.

"Oh, for God's sake, Royce, tell me it isn't you."

His stomach began to churn, and he regretted the shots of schnapps he'd sipped as a pregame bracer.

"No," she said. "You're shitting me! Oh Jesus, I can't believe it."

Suddenly, it all slammed down on him. Here he was, a man, a grown man, dressed in a blue chicken suit, in front of 2,000 people. And this was his job. In all of human history, had anybody ever been a bigger idiot?

He staggered away from the refreshment stand and toward his RV.

"BUBBA!"

A ten year old boy, no doubt wired on Cracker Jacks and a half gallon of Coke, stood in his path. "SLAP ME FIVE, DUDE!"

"Get the fuck out of my way," Royce said, pushing past the kid and making a beeline for the Kountry Kamper RV. There was a bottle of Mescal sitting on the coffee table, and it was calling Royce Perry's name.

JUST before sunrise, Royce came to with a godawful stench packed into his nostrils and the very sound of his throbbing temples echoing around him in the dark. When he reached up to scratch his cheek, he bumped into the cowl of Bubba the Blue Hen, and the oddness of it triggered memories of the night before. As it turned out, dropping into the Cork and Bottle in a blue hen costume was a sure way to get the free drinks flowing. He dimly recalled a jury-rigged tubing system that had enabled him to suck shots directly from a glass without removing Bubba's cowl. And just as he got a chuckle over that, despite the pain, he remembered the worst of it. With a cold fear, he reached out across the bed and, sure enough, discovered a naked thigh that most certainly belonged to someone not himself.

"Fuck." The word echoed hollowly in the cowl, like the voice of the Lord.

Slowly, he raised his body off the bed. The cowl had turned itself backward during the night, and he slowly pivoted the eye-holes into position; as they aligned, Royce scanned a series of Brad Paisley posters and a cheap pine bookshelf with a Mickey Mouse digital alarm clock, a book of Suzanne Somers' poetry, and a box of rubbers, opened, before stopping finally on a brace of tits that were unmistakable, given the presence of a double nipple on each. Marsha Wiltz. Son of a bitch. Rainey would have a ten-gallon fit. For better than a decade, the youngest of the three Wiltz daughters had blazed a sweaty trail through Brampton and surrounding burghs, leading with those double-barreled freaks of nature, which neither man nor woman would admit a hunger for though many had tasted. Marsha was nothing if not convenient, less particular than your average Irish setter, and prone to outright kink; Bubba's costume had undoubtedly provoked her, and the gods of alcohol had driven Royce to her lair, a secondhand house trailer at the end of Portal Road.

The Mickey Mouse clock read a quarter past five, and Marsha snored like a bucket loader; it was time to make an escape. As quietly as he could, Royce sat up, which went no better than he expected. Tequila spins hit him, and he reeled up a grotty belch. The cowl filled with fumes that, had a spark been handy, might well have ignited, and his mouth pooled molar-deep in saliva. Then the headrush came and he bent double, closed his eyes, and slowly breathed. In. Out. Repeat. After a few rounds, he was ready to stand.

Naked from the neck down, he followed a scatter of blue feathers out the bedroom door and down the trailer's narrow hall to the living room. His boxer shorts had vanished, or perhaps even melted, but he found his feathered jumpsuit on the floor of the kitchen, with his wallet and car keys in the inside pocket. He tugged the suit on, and stepped out of the trailer into the dim light of dawn. Bubba's yellow feet lay like a pair of discarded toy rakes in the yard. He scooped them up and walked barefoot toward his Tercel, the idea of an ice-cold Coke and half a dozen aspirins dancing in his head. And that's when he noticed her sitting on the Tercel's hood.

"Rainey?"

"The same," she said sliding down to the gravel. "At least one of us is recognizable." She wore faded Levis, a flannel shirt with the sleeves cut short, and her powder-blue Chuck Taylors. Without the Hens cap, her straight red hair hung across part of her face, but didn't hide her grin.

"Look," Royce stuttered. His blood pumped furiously, threatening to burst at least three or maybe more critical vessels inside the seething eggshell of his skull. "The reason I'm over here is…"

Just then, Mr. Britches sprang from the window of Rainey's VW, hit the ground with his paws churning and charged toward the giant blue hen, yapping like he'd eaten a handful of speed. He leapt up and caught Royce mid-thigh, snagged a swatch of feathers, and hit the ground in a rolling explosion of blue.

"Britches," Royce said. "For Christ sake, it's me."

The shi-tzu, unbelieving, prepped for another strafing.

"Royce?," Rainey said. "Can you lose the bird head?"

He did. And then the full scent of her washed over him, and

he was poleaxed again. Jesus God. He knew the softness of that flannel shirt, knew that behind her tiredly drawn lips was the snaggle-toothed smile that had first won him over, that day long ago outside the Brampton Library, when she'd sworn to god she had no idea who he was or what position he played on the ball team, and he knew she was telling the truth.

"Look, Rainey," he said, "that girl doesn't mean shit to me." Rainey waved him off.

"I don't care," Rainey said. "You're both consenting, and it's your business, not mine."

Those words hurt.

"The fact is," she continued, "I came here to say I'm sorry. I didn't mean to make fun of you. So don't take it that way. It's just that seeing your ex standing next to you in a giant blue hen suit is not what you expect out of life."

"Don't say 'ex,' Rainey. Please." The thought of touching her flanneled shoulders made him woozy.

"I didn't come here to talk about that, Royce."

"But what else is there to talk about?"

"Nothing. I just know how you are. I didn't want your feelings to get hurt because I laughed. But I think it's good you got a job.

"With benefits," Royce said. "Full medical. And you know what, Rainey? You know why I took that job?"

"That's the wrong reason, Royce," she said. "You need to do better for yourself, not for me."

"For us," Royce said. And he felt his stomach start to churn. "So you can get rid of that fuckin' shortstop and come back home."

For just a shadow of a moment, she hesitated. This was not tequila-induced hallucination; this was real. All she had to do was take one step toward him—and she would, he could feel it. One step, and all this holy hell was over.

"That's the way," he said, stretching out his fluffy blue

wings. "You and Britches can head out and I'll follow you home in the Toyota. We'll go over to your mother's and pick up the rest of your stuff later."

No girl Royce had ever seen smiled quite like Lorraine Dewley. The first time he saw her do it—and every time after— it sneaked onto her face. One tiny corner of her lip bent slightly upward, and a dimple bloomed above it that was perfect enough to break his heart. Then her green eyes seemed to haze over a bit, and you could tell she was thinking about why she was smiling, just turning it over once in her mind. Finally, the haze disappeared and the smile bloomed fully, her lips turned up at both ends and the snaggle tooth peeked out, and her whole face shone. Royce had seen the transformation so many times he should have been immune to it. But always, it thrilled him.

This time, though, her smile was different. That thinking pause lasted longer, and the smile that came after was bittersweet.

"I'd like to, Royce," Rainey said. "At least part of me would. But I just can't. I promised Stephen I'd meet him for breakfast at Annie's." And she took a step away.

He should have said something. He should have said anything. Instead, he carried the hen cowl to his Tercel and lashed it on the roof rack, not bothering to turn when he heard the familiar scratch of the VW's ignition, or even to take one last look as Rainey drove out of sight. Back at the apartment, Royce stripped off the jumpsuit, pulled all the shades, set the AM radio on the morning oldies, and crawled into the nest of blankets on the sofa. The blackness he fell into was the most welcome he could remember.

WHEN he'd dropped off, the situation had seemed piss-poor to worse, but with twelve hours' sleep, two cigarettes, a bowl of Cap'n Crunch and half a pitcher of iced tea, extra sweet, Royce could see a brighter side. Rainey'd come to see him, no doubt behind the shortstop's back. And when he'd asked her to come home, she hadn't turned him down outright, but with a pinch of regret. Most important, even if the shortstop hadn't taken a poke at him when Royce as much called his mother a whore, he'd cringed, sure as hell. And cringe was just a notch below crumble.

Still, as the Hens limped through the last of June, Royce couldn't seem to push VanSkyver over. He rode the shortstop as hard as he could without being obvious, but crumble never entered the picture. Once, on a road trip to Massachusetts, Royce thought he'd finally broken the son of a bitch. Van Skyver had ridden a 1-19 batting slump into Fall River, where he struck out swinging hard on an 0-2 changeup that a tenth grader could've parked.

"Nice cut," Bubba squawked as the shortstop jogged onto the field for the next inning.

Blood leapt into VanSkyver's face, and he whirled on Bubba and charged. Royce made ready to shuck his wings, a maneuver he'd rehearsed repeatedly in the welding shop parking lot. When the shortstop went off, he intended to get in a lick or two—purely as self-defense, of course. And why not? The players got full medical, too, so they were both covered. And he'd never been in a fight that lasted more than two or three punches. But before VanSkyver could take the first swing, Jimmy McAnallan, the Hens' third baseman, jumped in, bear-hugged him, and dragged him back toward short. This detour Royce hadn't considered; it had never occurred to him that a neutral third party might queer his plan. Worse, by inning's end, Van Skyver had calmed down, and was ready to talk. But what he said, Royce didn't want to hear.

As the Hens' first hitter stepped into the batting box, VanSkyver exited the dugout. He walked over to Royce, who leaned against the batting cage, trying to pick some decent looking cooter out of the crowd.

"Listen, Perry," the shortstop said. "I understand why you might be angry about this. But it's between you and Lorraine, not you and me. I don't think you're a bad guy. Honest. So why don't you just leave me alone?"

That only made Royce try harder. But the shortstop went back to ignoring everything he did to piss him off.

Royce worked Rainey hard too. When he circulated through the crowd, Bubba the Blue Hen focused as much attention on her as on all the other fans combined. If this made VanSkyver jealous, he never showed it—another disappointment—but it did succeed in pissing off Bruford Allen.

"Royce," Bruford said, "you know I've always liked you." It was the evening of the Fourth of July fireworks, with rockets and spanglers and other assorted doodads exploding over Blue Hen Field. "But what you got to understand is that I'm payin' you to entertain all the fans, not just the ones you want to fuck. Now, you can do the job, or I can fire your ass and get somebody else. And you know as well as I do that there's a half-dozen idiots around here who'd be glad to be Bubba, especially with the medical."

For a moment Royce considered ditching it all. But then he caught the sound of Rainey's voice as she oohed over a sky-rocket, and he knew he couldn't give up—at least not yet.

"Sure thing, B.A.," he said. "Fair is fair." But that wasn't strictly a promise. As soon as was feasible, he'd be back to hounding Rainey full time.

Still, for all the trouble it stirred, Royce's attention to Rainey did him little good. No matter what strategy he tried, she killed it with the deadliest weapon known to woman—treating him like a friend. In their space on the bleachers, with the smell of Charlie's Charco Dogs and her bubblegum shampoo spicing the air, they talked about summer, and work, and Rainey's dad's prostate, and Cindy Howard's DWI, and all sorts of other crap that as far as Royce was concerned added up to nothing. Which he happened to mention one evening in early August, as the Hens took the field for the second game of a double header against the Bath Ironmen.

Rainey chewed on his comment a minute, curling a knot of sunpaled amber hair around her index finger and staring off toward somewhere beyond center field.

"If you don't want to talk with me, Royce," she said finally, "what do you want to live with me for?" And she turned toward him with a greeneyed gaze that made his feathers tremble.

Later, back at his apartment, Royce shed his Bubba suit and collapsed on the couch in a state of near-catatonia. It was the first week in August, and the regular season ended in the second. The Hens' playoffs hopes were the same as they always were—completely nonexistent. That gave him seven days to pull it off; after that it would be decision time for Rainey and the shortstop. Would Stephen J. VanSkyver move into Brampton full time, and get a place with Rainey? Or worse yet, would he go back where he came from and take her along? Either way, the odds would only get longer. Royce tried not to panic. He'd been in some tight spots before, on the field and off. And he'd discovered that sometimes, it was just a matter of hanging in and waiting for your pitch.

Midway through the fourth beer of the evening, as he watched an old episode of Batman on his tiny Sanyo TV, the pitch came. This was bold, and he couldn't do it alone, but there wasn't any alternative that he could figure. Which meant, if you looked at it right, that he had no other choice. He went to the kitchen table, picked up the phone, and dialed the number he'd written on the wall two months before. The phone rang for quite a while, but eventually it picked up.

"Hey, Donnie," Royce said into the receiver. "It's the bird man. I'm havin' a little trouble with this Bubba thing. Think you could give me some help?"

IN a corner booth at Annie's Pancake Shack that Saturday morning, Royce explained the whole shebang—Rainey and the baby, the full medical benefits, and the campaign to get Stephen J. VanSkyver tossed out of the henhouse.

Donnie took a swallow of his Orange Fanta and poked at his scrambled eggs. Behind his milky lenses, he blinked in disbelief.

"Jesus, Royce. You are a fuckup."

"Easy, D. I'm tender here."

"I'll say. Tender in the head. Didn't you read the player guide?" Donnie said.

"Fuck, D. Does anybody read it besides you?"

"Well, I know somebody that should have, Royce. Cause if you did, you'd've found out that your shortstop is a Buddhist."

"A what?"

"A Buddhist. He's pacified, Royce. He'll never fight you back, no matter what you do."

Fuck and a dogturd. Was he the unluckiest man on the face of the earth?

Donnie thoughtfully chewed for a moment. "You know," he said, his voice mumbled by a clot of scrambled eggs. "Whyn't you just come out and give her what she wants? Paint a big sign that says 'Dear Rainey. I want to knock you up. Love Royce.' Hire a plane to pull it over the ballpark. Shit, I don't know. I mean, maybe she doesn't even deserve you. She's a good girl, Royce. So clean yourself up. Get a real job. And give her a goddam engagement ring. You know as well as I do, the bottom line is that Rainey loves you. This shortstop is just a peccadillo." As soon as the word came out, Donnie smiled.

"Great," Royce said. "I ask for some advice and I get Mr. Vocabulary."

Donnie scooped up the last of his eggs. "Have it your way,

100

Royce," he said. "You always do." He took another swallow of his Fanta, slid out of the booth, and headed for the door.

All right. Fine. There were times when you promised anything, and this was one.

"D?"

Donnie stopped.

"You help me, and I swear," Royce said, although he was simultaneously aware that he was likely lying. "That on Monday morning, I will go bright and early to that god damn cement plant and ask for a job."

"Swear?"

Royce held up his palm, and Donnie slid back into the booth.

"All right," Royce said. "We don't have a shitload of time here. But I got an idea."

FROM Royce's point of view, the Buddhist thing seemed fishy. Every one he'd ever known had converted for one reason—to get more pussy by appearing sincere—and it seemed to him that might likely be the case with Stephen J. VanSkyver. Rainey'd always been a pushover for sincerity—show her a TV show about somebody who went to India to save some orphans, and she'd be sobbing one minute and ready to screw the next.

So if VanSkyver was faking it, the thing to do was up the ante, big time. And even if he wasn't, what the hell else was there? Which is why, just 15 minutes before game time on a hot August evening at Blue Hen Field, Royce, dressed in full Bubba regalia, was following Donnie Lyaski's pudgy ass up a telephone pole and onto the roof of the announcer's booth, where they ducked behind a billboard for Hank Blevins' Chevrolet and waited for H-hour.

The view from the top was perfect. The stands were packed with a full house, Rainey in the front row of the bleachers, and victory in the air. Puffing and red-faced after the climb, Donnie crouched on one knee, squinting through his bulging lenses in the slowly setting sun.

"Royce Perry, you are fucking crazy," Donnie hissed, though with the loudspeaker blaring an ad for the Brampton House of Pants no one else on Earth could hear him. "And I am, too, for going along with this. It'll never work in a million years."

"Naysayer."

"B.A. will fire your ass."

Royce smiled. "Well, hell, Donnie. I'll have a new job come Monday."

Royce stood up slightly and peeked around the billboard. The steel cable they'd strung the night before hadn't been noticed—at least not yet. It ran from the telephone pole where they stood to a light tower beyond the left field fence. And it intersected perfectly with the area between second and third base where shortstop Stephen J. VanSkyver plied his trade. Royce picked up the trapeze and pulley from the roof of the booth, climbed up the stepstool they'd stored against the back of the billboard, and clipped the trapeze onto the cable. Then he sat back down, leaned against the billboard and lit a cigarette.

"Royce..."

Royce held up a wing. "Just let me enjoy a moment of reflection, here, D."

What thoughts fill a man's head in his moment of truth? For Royce it was, like it always had been: Lorraine Dewley. He closed his eyes, and faded into the blackness of Bubba's cowl. Why was it so hard to give her what she wanted? Would it be that bad? A steady job with benefits, and a decent paycheck? A wife to come home to and maybe a kid? What would that lose him? But then the other side of the argument stepped in, and it stepped in hard on the side of freedom. Royce Perry didn't have a whole lot, but he didn't need a whole lot if he had that. No plans, and no cares. Days in the welding shop as his own boss, and nights at the Cork and Bottle, shooting pool and draining beers. If only Rainey would come back. And maybe when she'd seen this next trick, she would.

"Psssst! Royce. "The color guard is lining up." He saw Donnie peeking in through Bubba's eye hole.

All right. This was the time. All the fans had risen. And on the field, Stephen J. VanSkyver had turned to face the flagpole in center field, his Hens cap clasped behind his back.

Royce stood up and climbed the stepstool, swung his feathered legs over the top of the billboard and took a seat, grasped the bars of the trapeze. At the last minute, as the band struck the first notes of the Star Spangled Banner, he took off Bubba's cowl and tossed it down to Donnie. This time, he wanted the shortstop to look him in the eye.

It took Royce a moment to settle his beating heart, and then he pushed off, swung down onto the trapeze bars, and dropped from the placid blue sky like a hen out of hell.

They had tested the rig the night previous, using a 60-lb. bag of sand, and it had worked flawlessly. But now, as he plunged toward the field with rapid acceleration, Royce realized that they should have used a more realistic weight. At 165, he sagged the wire at a much steeper curve, which made the descent much faster, and the path of his glide a hair low. Raising his scaly feet, he barely cleared the bayonets of the color guard, and settled in at impact level thirty feet from his target. The anthem singer's voice petered to silence. The band clattered to a halt. And Stephen J. Van Skyver turned to face his fate.

"MOTHERFUCKERRRRRRR!!!!!!!!"

Royce screamed at the top of his lungs, then melted into a dreamy haze that enveloped him like his mother's arms. He sagged on the trapeze like a rag doll, tired to the bone. Tired of drinking and smoking weed. Tired of welding shitbox cars and getting paid in cash. Tired of being a has-been jock. And tired of the Royce Perry legend in all its forms. But most of all, he was tired of being alone, because that's what you were when you stood belly to the bar, cigarette in one hand and Budweiser in the other, with everyone around who thought they knew you and loved you but didn't do either. And now Royce understood that, and something else too—that Rainey knew him and loved him both, and he would do anything to get her back. Even benefits. Even jobs. And even babies.

A true gamer, and none too bright into the bargain, Stephen J. VanSkyver crouched, raised his mitt, and made to catch the birdman who dove toward him at a speed now well into double digits. At impact, Royce felt the satisfying snap of VanSkyver's wrist as it bent back onto itself, then a fiery rip of pain as the shortstop's front teeth sank into his thigh. The trapeze disconnected and Royce swung wildly up and right, tumbling like a feathered comet toward second base; he landed on his shoulder, which popped from the socket like a cork from a bottle. His head hit the dirt and the world exploded in a sparky festoon.

How long he was out Royce never knew. But he was an athlete still, and the first notion he had upon coming to was to get up and let people know he was OK. His ears rang, a low-pitched drone, but beyond that was total silence, which he found normal, because he was hurt, and the crowd would be waiting for him to show motion before they could applaud. And who was he to disappoint them?

Royce raised up on one elbow, and his eyes defocused, them came clear. It was the funniest thing: he was wrapped in a blanket of blue feathers, which he just could not figure. He blinked, shook his head and waved at the crowd, which began to clap, slowly, and then, as they recognized him, in an increasing tumult that shook the stadium's metal roof, drifted out over the river and to the town of Brampton beyond. It was a moment of glory, and Royce might have stood up, but instead he waited, because he knew she'd be there. And then, suddenly, she was. Rainey Dewley. Busted out of the stands and running toward him. Toward him, just like every time before, and yelling his name.

Melting

Mr. Schuller and his child bride live at the Igloo Fill-n-Rest. Thousands of motorists pass the Igloo Fill-n-Rest every day without stopping. They are too far up the hill on the highway. They are too close to the new hotel and twenty pump gas station. The igloos ("Cabins $8. 2 Beds, Sink, Toilet," the sign reads) are closed, except for one of the eight. Mr. Schuller and his child bride live in #4.

At one time, Mr. Robinson, Mr. Schuller's long dead uncle, tried dressing his pump jockeys in realistic Esquimo clothing. The Igloo Fill-n-Rest is located eighty miles southeast of Los Angeles. Instead of automobiles lined up at his pumps, Mr. Robinson got ambulances.

Now Mr. Robinson is gone; it is just Mr. Schuller and his child bride. Their days vary but are never busy. The evenings are always the same. In the evening, Mr. Schuller's child bride walks through the crumbling asphalt courtyard of the Igloo Fill-n-Rest. She arches the hot soles of her feet, brushing them over dewy grassblooms that push up through the broken macadam. She walks very gracefully and sways a bit, as if she were singing, but she never sings. She has never heard a song. Mr. Schuller's child bride is deaf and mute.

Mr. Schuller never takes walks in the courtyard; he's seen it so many times that it hurts him to have to look at it again, empty and dark. When it's time to close down the Igloo Fill, Mr. Schuller walks out behind Igloo #4 to the big rusty fuse box nailed to the old, leaning-over telephone pole, opens it, and smashes down the red-handled breaker switch. When he does this, all the lights in the courtyard go off. All the frogs in the old, greenwater-filled wading pool at the back end of the courtyard stop singing for a few seconds and the dark is heavy with quiet. After those few seconds of darkness and silence, Mr. Schuller smashes the big breaker switch back on.

When the lights in the Igloo Fill-n-Rest's courtyard go off, then back on again, someone, maybe someone on their way to Old Mexico or Illinois, an old man or a young woman, or two teenage boys courting the summer night in a stolen Camaro from LA, will think they saw a flash of lightning and start fantasizing about thunderstorms.

When the lights in the courtyard go off, then back on again, Mr. Schuller's child bride turns from her walk as quickly as the greasy frogs stop singing in the wading pool, and walks back to the front of the lot where two red and green gas pumps stand like rusty Buckingham Palace guards. Mr. Schuller, who is turning off the pumps and squinting through a gauzy yellow flashlight beam at the numbers that indicate the gasoline sales of the day, copies the figures into an oil-smudged pocket notebook with the fat nub of a silver pencil. Years ago, Mr. Schuller cheated on the figures, but has since stopped. The numbers mean nothing to him now.

Big-bodied moths ricochet like powdered bullets off the steel hooded lamps that hang above the doorways of the cabins. Sometimes they hiss if they hit the bulbs, but Mr. Schuller's child bride cannot hear them. She cannot hear her husband's small scratching against the notebook. She watches. When he puts the notebook in the front pocket of his shirt beneath the round white patch with the red star, she takes his hand. They walk together to the rusty fuse box and turn out the lights in the courtyard. The Igloo Fill-n-Rest settles into another night with its lovers in each other's arms.

It was not always this way. Mr. Schuller's child bride came to the Igloo Fill-n-Rest seventeen years before. She arrived at

Mr. Schuller's Buckingham Palace pumps in a rusty Buick station wagon that her father had driven across the country from Brown Springs, Arkansas.

They worked the farms, picking fruits and vegetables all across the South, season after season; her mother and father, aunts, uncles, and cousins. All in the station wagon. Always too many. Too many colicky babies. Too many dying old women. Too many cousins and uncles who touched her too much. Mr. Schuller's child bride was thirteen then; too pretty to be living in the migrant camps without being touched. She couldn't hear and couldn't speak and her auburn hair held thick about her white shoulders like wind-twisted curtains of cloudburst rain. She hated the men who crawled across the rotten floors of the fruit-picking camps and the cracked, stuffing-crumble seats of the Buick to rub against her until they wet.

When the wagon pulled into the Igloo Fill-n-Rest, it had seen the whole of Arizona in a day, non-stop. The babies had peed their diapers and everyone else had sweat out their water. The children's faces were branded in patterns of hot vinyl, and no one had eaten a meal since New Orleans. There were eleven of them in the Buick; three men, four women, four children.

The child bride's father and uncles together had barely enough money for gas and it was well past dark and time to sleep. Even though the men were very tall, the tiny igloos looked good to them. The child bride's father swung open the door of the Buick and pumped his own gas. He handed some filthy dollar bills to Mr. Schuller.

"Texaco! Thank Jesus! You can always find a Texaco." Her father held Mr. Schuller's hand for a moment after shaking it, like he was a very dear friend. "But I bet you don't always find travelers as sorry as us. We come all the way from Gallup, New Mexico today."

The child bride's father took off a disintegrating grey base-ball cap and held it at his waist, leaned toward Mr. Schuller and whispered through his thick red moustache.

"My wife's sister Charlotte died in Chula Vista and we're goin' to the funeral. We're, uh, I'm kind of embarrassed to say it, but we're kind of in rough shape. Things ain't exactly easy for work in West Arkansas. If we could just get a place to lay down, me and my brother in laws'll work like the devil for ya' in the mornin'. Whatever ya' got."

Mr. Schuller assented, and was awakened before daylight by the sound of the station wagon bellowing off into the dark. By the time he could've roused the constable, they would've been long gone. People like that knew how to hide.

That afternoon, Mr. Schuller was doing some patching on the roof of Igloo #7 when the child bride wandered past his ladder, as beautiful and silent as snow. Mr. Schuller wasted no time in getting her to the constable's office, where no one had a clue as to who she was. That was 1953, and there was a war. There was a surplus of orphans, and no one wanted any more, so Mr. Schuller took the girl home.

Less than two years later, she came to his bed. It was autumn and dark at 8:00 and she came to him quietly and took off the blue cotton blouse that he'd bought her from the profits of the Igloo Fill-n-Rest. He saw that she was as lithe and soft as all the women he'd ever dreamed about all alone in the bed of Igloo #4. He was forty-seven and had never made love to a woman; the child bride was his first.

They'd gotten married soon after. Mr. Schuller had seen enough movies to know that he had to make an honest woman out of the girl. In the living room of #4, they were married by the constable. No one attended the ceremony. Her family, of course, was gone, and Mr. Schuller didn't have any people either.

They were quite happy for several years. Mr. Schuller's child bride learned to cook, and they turned Igloo #6 into a breakfast counter. Travelers came to know the Igloo Fill-n-Rest.

In the spring of 1958, two very alarming things happened. A huge highway appeared, building its way forward with men and machines, on the hill above the Igloo Fill-n-Rest. Mr. Schuller's child bride became pregnant. She didn't know what it was, this feeling of urgency. It made her want to run away and stay put at the same time. She was afraid, and she wanted Mr. Schuller around to make her feel safe. Already, though, Mr. Schuller was gone. The grunting of the machines and the thick bands of concrete arrested him. He sat in an oil-colored wooden chair outside by the Texaco pumps and watched as the highway built itself across the top of the hill and down the other side, out of sight.

The highway began to take travelers away from the Igloo Fill. Only the cars of vacationers loyal to Mr. Schuller and his child bride stopped and stayed, and then even those were gone. There was a big new hotel up on the highway. It was more expensive, but it had features. Features like showers. Air conditioning. A swimming pool. Twenty shiny steel and chrome gas pumps. But Mr. Schuller refused to blame the lack of customers on the hotel. It was the highway. "Those bastards," he'd snarl. "They had to run that goddam highway so far up the hill that no one can see me." The Igloo Fill-n-Rest, he fretted, had become invisible.

One morning in June, when the frogs in the wading pool were just dropping their tails and starting to make land excursions, he began to repaint the cabins in a shade of white so brilliant that it made the child bride's teeth ache. Mr. Schuller couldn't afford a gigantic steel tower covered in neon like the one that advertised the hotel, but he could afford paint. With enough paint, the travelers would see him. It was the whitest paint that the child bride had ever seen. It fairly flashed as he smacked it on, madly, cursing the whole time.

Mr. Schuller's child bride heard nothing, but all the whiteness scared her. Her sickness scared her as well. She began to be awake when she had used to want to sleep and she hardly slept at all. She vomited constantly and couldn't stand the heat. She was glad that no one came to the Igloo Fill-n-Rest. The sight of the grill and smell of the grease made her nauseous. She needed Mr. Schuller close to her. Mr. Schuller only cursed and painted.

And painted some more. He troweled on more white paint and more again, certain that those on the highway would notice. They did not. He painted the cabins another coat. And another. June passed, swirled away into the heat like a mirage on the highway. July. A third coat. He painted from sunlight to darkness and sometimes after, by the light of the steel-shaded lamps.

Mr. Schuller's hands grew callouses and he smelled of kerosene. Exhausted, he fell into bed next to his child bride, never noticing the fear and abandonment in her eyes. Never noticing that she did not sleep. He fell asleep with the highway in his ears. Headlights creased his dreams.

August. A morning so hot that the frogs in the wading pool showed only their nares above the waterline and scarcely croaked. Mr. Schuller was painting madly, cursing and sweating, when he noticed her. The child bride stood beneath the ladder like the first day he'd seen her, silent and smiling. Her freshly cut wrists sprayed sticky roseblooms onto the walls of Cabin #2. Blood ran down the walls like moonlight.

Mr. Schuller leapt from the ladder. The first time he hit her, her lip spat blood onto the cabin wall, and that made him angrier. He didn't know that she had a baby inside her. Her belly was no bigger than if she'd swallowed a gumdrop. It may not have mattered if he had; the white paint was ruined. Mr. Schuller hit the child bride, and hit her again. When she lay on the ground and did not move, he called an ambulance. The Igloo Fill-n-Rest was not surprised. It had seen ambulances before.

Mr. Schuller's child bride stayed in the hospital for some time. Her husband kept on painting. On the third day of her stay, sympathetic nurses, using pencil drawings and nearly-futile sign language, explained to the child bride that she'd lost a baby. They told Mr. Schuller as well. He responded by painting furiously. There was no interview with the police or a social worker. This was a small town in Southern California. This was 1958.

When the bruises on the child bride's face began to turn from martin blue to yellow and green, the nurses put her in a taxi and sent her back to the Igloo Fill-n-Rest. She hated Mr. Schuller but was not afraid of him. She wondered if he was still painting.

He was. When the child bride got out of the yellow taxicab and saw her husband, he had just finished with the last of the igloo cabins, Igloo #8. He walked over to the taxi slowly, shirtless, his growing-older body hanging off his bones like Hiroshima. Mr. Schuller had painted all of the cabins as black as a widow's glove. When the child bride saw what he had done, she loved him again.

And loves him to this day. People on the highway now notice the Igloo Fill-n-Rest, on their way to Georgia, on their way from Abilene and Old Mexico. People drive by and the cabins catch their eye. They never stop. They only think. "What are those eight black mounds down there, like giant coal-colored gumdrops soaking up the sun?" they think. But they never stop to find out.

night. the switch. off. on. the child bride's arched foot. the smudge of the pencil nub. sleep.

Lucky Duck, Lucky Luck

Before the tiny, homely package arrived in the mail that morning, Ann believed herself to be one of the luckiest people in Jasper, North Carolina. Didn't Stephen, her handsome, prosperous husband of twenty years, think the world of her? Wasn't their daughter, Angela, now approaching seventeen, as popular as she was pretty and as intelligent as she was both, much the same as Ann had been? And wasn't Ann respected throughout the community as a devoted mother and a loyal wife?

Even the unpleasant part of her past—and there was really only one—had been left forever behind; the city of Jasper had given her a new start and she'd gotten over her troubles, in large part due to Stephen, who'd stood by her resolutely and without complaint.

Ann lived a life of means. Stephen had parlayed a small sum bequeathed him by his father into Jasper's most prominent realty business, enabling Ann, at least while Angela was at school, to spend her time doing whatever pleased her. She worked three days a week at the reception desk of the Cayette County Historical Society—which gave her a chance to catch up on her reading, as much as anything else. At home, she spent hours online, spelunking through her ancestry. She drowsed through the morning newspaper, lingered over coffee. Other people lived busier lives, lives full of work and complicated relationships, but Ann managed to avoid this troublesome business. Lucky duck, lucky luck, she often said to herself, as she did that morning, brushing her long blonde hair in front of the bathroom mirror. She looked good, she thought, for a woman of 46, despite the weight she'd put on over the past year, and the occasional sneaked cigarette.

Ann had already checked the mailbox once that morning, although she wasn't expecting anything unusual. Occasionally, she ordered beauty supplies (retinol for crow's feet; herbal salve for the pouches under her eyes) or picked something up on QVC on those few nights when Stephen worked late. But since he'd warned her that her spending had gotten reckless, she'd resisted her urges for some time.

At a little after ten, the letter carrier, a young man Ann viewed as one of her closest friends, strode up the brick walkway to the heavy oak door. Ann swung it open to greet him.

"Good morning, Henry."

"Hey, Mrs. Clark," he said, "Nice morning, right?" He pulled a fist-sized, kraft-paper parcel from his satchel. The package was battered, its corners jammed in by collision so that it was more ball-shaped than cubical, spackled in floridly canceled five-cent stamps, and addressed in spindly, uneven blue ballpoint to "Ann Marie Clark, Sanders Circle, Jasper."

"Took a while for this one to get here," Henry said. "They had it up in Raleigh for a few months and Chapel Hill before that. Sorry about that. Some people just don't understand how to use a Zip Code."

Still, the very fact of the package thrilled her. She took it to the dim sanctuary of the kitchen, set it in the middle of the softly gleaming cherry table. With the tips of her fingers, she gently caressed its seams and ridges, imagined what it might be and who might have sent it. She recalled that lovely man she'd met at the historical society in June, with whom she'd traded addresses on the pretense of sharing information about steam railway carriages. She cupped the package in her hand and sniffed gently, probing for the warm, citrusy scent of the stranger's cologne.

Her fingers trembled as she picked at the corner of a strip of packing tape with a ginger-lacquered nail; the paper crackled warmly as it unfolded. Inside was a small, wooden box redolent not of the citrus, but of lilies of the valley; it surprised her that she recognized the scent. She lifted the lid, tugged out a packet of pale yellow tissue, light as the body of a sparrow, tied with a soft, gold-glittered cord. Ann tugged gently at the knot, which slipped open with a tender hiss and a spray of glitter that pixied the morning light. *Lucky duck*, Ann whispered, *lucky luck*.

She reached inside the tissue cocoon, let the pads of her fingertips read the object like Braille. It was flawlessly smooth, convex on the top and concave below; she imagined the stranger from the historical society walking along a deserted Caribbean beach, searching for the perfect shell. But as she traced the object further, another vision arose. Acid sharped the back of her tongue; she lost her balance for just a second and caught herself, leaned against the table. When she had regained herself, she lifted the object in a clenched fist, took a deep breath, and opened her hand. Keenly polished and utterly impassive, a glass eye regarded her from the cradle of her palm.

ANN remembered what had happened as the purest of accidents. A group of girls, high school juniors then. A cabin Ann's father had built for her in the woods behind their house in Safford's Falls, her hometown. A windy night in October, a game of hide and go seek, and a horrible tragedy—Myra Coggins, one of Ann's best friends, had hit a tree branch running for home base and lost an eye. There had been accusations, friendships severed, brief but nasty litigation.

Now, all of it had returned, carried to her doorstep in a tiny, forlorn package. Heat rising to her face and her heart pounding, Ann traced a circuit around the fawn-colored iris with her index finger, turned the piece turtle and settled the meat of her thumb into the object's incurved back, where it had once mated with the socket of Myra Coggins' left eye. She felt bewilderment above all. After all these years, how could it all come back?

ANN didn't bother with her cell; Stephen never answered when he was at the work, and seldom responded to messages, no matter how urgent. She took the Volvo and drove to his office herself.

The receptionist, a sturdy woman in her late fifties whom Ann didn't recognize, was reading a magazine when she arrived. By then Ann was frantic; she wanted to pound on the door of Stephen's office, but she knew how he felt about privacy, so she waited, paced, her thumb working sweatily on the concave back of the eye, which she held deep in the pocket of her faded nylon windshell.

"I'm here," Ann said finally.

"Pardon me?" The receptionist slowly looked up.

"I need to see Stephen right away."

The woman put down her magazine and picked up the phone, but before she could punch in an extension, Stephen came down the back hall from another office. In the dim light of the hallway, his silhouette looked unfamiliar; Ann tried, but couldn't seem to recall the sheer physical power he'd carried as a younger man, power that had made him an all-state linebacker twenty years before. He limped noticeably, the residue of an old knee injury, had put on weight over the summer. Is this the man I married, Ann wondered, and realized that it was.

"Stephen," Ann said, perhaps a little too loudly, and her husband turned his head. He looked older than she remembered, more worn out. She noticed fraying at the cuffs of his plum-colored Oxford shirt, a dull scuff at the toe of one shoe.

"Hey, Annie, is everything OK?" he said.

"I got a package in the mail today."

"Yeah?"

"From Myra Coggins," Ann said.

Before she could continue, Stephen put a hand on her upper arm, led her into his office, and quietly guided the door closed. He went to the window, turned on the box fan—not, she realized, to cool the room, but to create cover for their conversation.

Ann took the glass eye from the pocket of her windshell, set it gently on the top of the maple-veneer desk.

"There," she said.

Stephen stared at the glass eye in disbelief, ran his fingers through his thinning dark hair. "What the fuck. She's got no business starting up with this again. I mean, she did start it, didn't she? You didn't call her, Annie? Please tell me you didn't."

"How would I? Do you think I have her number?" She moved toward him, wanted more than anything for him to hold her, but he stepped away.

"You know where she is as well as I do," he said. "Still down there in White-trashville."

"Stephen, I grew up there. You know I don't like it when you talk that way."

"Really," he said. "You know what I don't like? I don't like when you barge in here in the middle of the workday, when I'm trying to get something important accomplished, and interrupt me."

"I didn't—"

"I don't like that you can't handle a simple prank pulled by a high school classmate from twenty years ago."

By then she was crying. "It's more than that," she said. "You know it is."

"Oh, Jesus," Stephen said. He put his arms around her, and she moved forward, pressed herself against his chest. "Look. I'm sorry," he said, "But I am freaked. You paid for what you did. You paid plenty. And if she's coming after us now, that would be bad, Annie. Really bad. Cause we got nothing to spare. Do you have any idea what the real estate market in Cayette County is like right now? She starts this up again, and the courts see it her way, we are screwed."

He went to his desk, tugged open a drawer and extracted a ragged sheet of yellow legal paper, scratched a number on it with a cheap ballpoint. A blade of sweat greased his cheek.

"Call Lonnie Wells. He'll put a scare in her, nip it in the bud."

"Your lawyer?"

"Just don't spend too much time on the phone. At two-fifty an hour, it adds up."

He pushed the yellow paper into her hand and headed for the office door. "I got a closing to get to, so I'll see you when I get home. And whatever you do, don't show that thing to anybody. We don't need the publicity."

Ann picked up the glass eye and slipped it back into her pocket, followed him out of the room and down the hall to the back door.

Stephen made it halfway across the parking lot before Ann gathered the courage to call after him.

"I was in the right back then," she said. "Wasn't I?"

Stephen stopped and turned. The late November sky had darkened, but shafts of light pierced the clouds, giving the parking lot a keen, plasmic glow. He hobbled back across the lot toward her, and hope welled up. He put his hands on her shoulders, squatted slightly, and looked her square in the eye.

"The story's the same old same old," he said. "Stick to it, just like you always have, and we can move on."

BY late that afternoon, Ann had begun to feel better. Lonnie Wells, the attorney, had done a good bit to untangle her nerves.

"A settlement is just that, Ann. And Myra Coggins settled well. If she didn't handle the money in a smart way, she'll be seen as undeserving of more. And if she did, she's competent, and she shouldn't need additional funds. I mean, she's made a living, right?"

Ann recalled that Myra had converted the field behind the Coggins house in Safford's Falls into flower beds, cobbled together a small greenhouse and a roadside stand. Not that Ann had followed the course of Myra Coggins' life, but Safford's Falls was her hometown, and she had reason to be there on occasion. She'd even driven past the flower stand once, just to see how it looked.

After her talk with Lonnie Wells, Ann mixed herself a pitcher of gin and tonic and headed for the screen porch. She liked to cozy up, secluded from the street, imagine other ways her life might have played out. But today her respite felt less like leaving her everyday world behind than hiding from it. There was that small, curved piece of glass, after all. She'd been unable to resist its provocations, had propped it up on the redwood picnic table in front of her next to the sweating pitcher of G&T. The placid amber iris seemed not to implicate her, exactly, but to raise questions just the same. Why hadn't Stephen been able to say that she had been in the right back then? She had been, hadn't she?

Looking back, Ann recalled that she had invited Myra Coggins to the sleepover out of kindness; perhaps Ann's mother had suggested it, because frankly, the girl had problems fitting in. Ann, on the other hand, had none; the weekly summer sleepovers in the cabin were the envy of all the girls in the neighborhood. Being invited meant something: the chance to gossip, smoke a forbidden Lucky Strike, perhaps, or tipple from a contraband pint of crème de menthe. One time, several older boys had sneaked in through the back of the property for an impromptu game of post office. So when Ann invited Myra Coggins, poor, pudgy Myra Mouse, with her ironed beige hair and her lumpy chest, her front teeth big as Chiclets, why wouldn't Myra be thrilled?

But was the scenario that Ann remembered accurate? She

picked up the glass eye, tumbled it from palm to palm while the gin seeped in. Another vision took shape: a knot of girls near the third floor lockers of the high school, some indignation. A girl whose boyfriend had spoken to Myra Coggins in the cafeteria. Myra had sent him a love note, which had been passed around like a disease. Someone hatched a plan for revenge—not to hurt Myra physically, of course, but to shame her enough to keep her in line. It wasn't anything terrible; what teenage girl hadn't been involved in that type of plot? This was the way girls in high school lived, a seethe of shifting alliances, manipulation, shunning, and shame.

RIGHT on schedule at 7:15, Ann heard the door slam, then Angela called her name; she was home from soccer practice, and Ann realized that she hadn't done a thing about dinner. A few minutes later, Angela appeared on the screen porch, a bologna sandwich and a bottle of Snapple in her hands. She'd pulled her wheat-colored hair back in a severe ponytail that highlighted cheekbones shadowed by her apple-green Abercrombie hoodie. She wore ecru Abercrombie slacks, and apple-green Nikes, no socks. Despite the updated clothing, Ann looked at her daughter and saw nothing more than herself at sixteen, wondered as always if Stephen's genetic complement were even involved.

"Wow, Mom. Big surprise finding you out here," Angela said by way of a greeting. "Drinks before dining?"

"Just one. How was your day, honey?"

"It sucked, mostly. There's this girl, Hannah Satterfield, who's a total idiot. And she tried to tell me that I couldn't talk to Rob Daniels, because apparently he'd hooked up with her one time, which he said he was totally hammered and I believe him, because it would be disgusting to get near something so fat, never mind the smell of the Salvation Army clothes she wears to try to make us believe she actually shops at American Eagle? So I told her to mind her own fucking business, and he wouldn't have got with her in the first place if he hadn't done seven shots of Jägermeister, although it was probably her looks that made him puke in the end, and she makes a big scene, sobbing all through geometry, which was totally ridiculous, and now Rob is pissed at me. Like it's not my fault you fucked a sea cow. Get over it."

Then Angela's fury deflated. "Oh my god," she said quietly. "What the fuck is that?"

Veiled in the gin, Ann fumbled for the glass eye, meaning to hide it, but it ricketed across the table and off, halfway across the tongue and groove floor of the porch.

"Mom?"

"It's um," Ann said, and suddenly she felt hopeless. As if a lawyer could make this go away. As if time and distance could.

"Jesus," Angela said. "The stories are true."

"What stories?"

"Never mind."

"I said, what stories? You tell me, God damn it."

"Don't go all fucking psycho on me. I said I don't know."

"You do," Ann said. "You do, because you said so."

"So I lied. Deal with it."

"Tell me!" Ann said. By then she was shouting. She lurched up from the table and grabbed Angela's shoulder, held her firmly and leaned into her face.

"All right," Angela said. "Last year, when we were at camp, Emma told me about that girl. The one who lost an eye. She said you were the gang leader. That's all."

Ann's hand dropped to her side.

"The gang leader. That's what Emma said about me?"

Angela nodded.

"And what did you tell her? Did you defend your mother?"

Angela gave a little grunt. "Defend you? I don't even know what happened. You never told me, Mom. What was I supposed to say?"

"And who told Emma? Her mom?" Cindy Pierce had been there the night of the accident. A bystander, but still.

"I don't know," Angela said. "I don't fucking KNOW!" She stomped back into the house, slamming the screen porch door. Ann heard footsteps quickly thudding over the worn pile carpet. The front door slammed, then silence. She poured another gin and tonic from the pitcher, took a swallow, then another. She waited almost an hour, hoping that Angela would come back, so she could tell her more of it. So she could explain. But the quiet remained. Finally, Ann went to hunt up her old address book.

CINDY Pierce had not been lucky in love. Between high school graduation and today, Ann recalled, she'd been married three times, her first husband taking up with their daughter's kindergarten teacher, her second dying of a heart attack on the tennis court at the Sylvan Oaks Club. The third husband had finally stuck. A jeweler by trade—was his name Connor, maybe? Mitchell? Ann had always pictured him as a tiny, fussy man, with a loupe in his eye socket and an impatient scowl. In truth, Ann was sure she had never met him, although they both now lived in Jasper. She and Cindy had parted after high school, and only saw each other occasionally, at the supermarket or across the pews in church, which Carl Pierce did not attend. Ann guessed there was a story there, and a juicy one, but today wasn't the day for that.

Ann found the correct number only after several tries; the drinks had blurred her focus a bit. She should have stopped earlier, she knew, but the glass eyes still lay there on the porch floor. What could she do with it, exactly? She considered throwing it in the trash, or more benignly, tossing it into the woods behind the house. But despite its inanimate nature, the sleek lozenge seemed impossible to simply discard. After a while, she slipped it into her purse, but the feeling didn't go away. Gin was the only solution she knew.

Cindy picked up the phone after just two rings. In minutes, it was just like the old days; tidbits of gossip and news about family, wonder over why they never got together for coffee or even dinner. It seemed like years since Ann had chatted this way with a friend, and she didn't want it to stop, but finally, she mentioned the package she'd received, what it contained, and where it had come from. The phone fell silent for a second. Cindy giggled.

"Omigod, that is priceless," she said. "Just priceless. I mean, after all these years. It's like she finally got you back, from the great beyond."

Ann's brain felt a little smudgy; as they'd talked, she'd put away the better part of another drink. She tried as best she could to keep things clear.

"Wait a minute," she said. "What do you mean, 'from the great beyond?'"

"Well, you know Myra Coggins died," Cindy said. "It's been a while, but I thought all of us knew. She got lymphoma. They gave her six months, but she was lucky. She made it almost a year and a half. It was last November, I think, a couple weeks before Thanksgiving."

"Oh my God," Ann said. "That's awful," but somewhere in the back of her mind she felt relief. There would be no lawsuit, no more court.

"It wasn't as bad as it could be," Cindy said. "She never got married, or had any kids, so it wasn't hard that way. And I heard she had friends around her all the time. From the flower business, I guess. They say her customers just adored her. Her sister moved back from Raleigh and took that over. She's living in the house…"

Quinine roiled in Ann's gut. She envisioned a chain of events that began with the accident: Myra Coggins' ruined eye, some x-rays. A few cells mutated by radiation, dormant for years and then suddenly, a tumor beginning to grow. She heard her own voice echoing over the line.

"Do they know what caused it?"

"For God's sake, Ann. It's the lottery," Cindy said. "They can say what they want. 'It's the chemicals. It's the food. It's genetic. It's being too fat.' The fact is, it's fucking cancer. Next time, it could be you. Could be me. But at least Myra kept her sense of humor. A glass eye. Jesus."

"I don't think it's funny."

"Well, shit, Ann. I guess you might not."

The phone line hummed.

"Did you tell Emma I was the gang leader that night?" Ann finally said.

"No, I did not."

"Well, somehow she's convinced that I instigated the thing. And I guess I know how she would think that; maybe she heard about the lawsuit. But I'd like it if you could tell her that other people were involved, too."

Ann heard the sound of her own blood, beating in her ear.

"Cindy?"

"Ann, we are way past the time of bullshit now. We sent a girl out into the woods at night, on a dare, because we wanted to make her look stupid. She had a choice, go or be an outcast. She went. Then we snuck up on her and scared her. She ran, and she hit a tree branch. Then we told everybody it was a game of hide and seek.

"We lied, Ann, but who wouldn't have? *She* lied, for Christ's sake, maybe not in court, but everywhere else, because even after what happened, she wanted to be our friend. The lying wasn't the crime. The planning of it was. The doing of it. The whole thing was hormones and teenage nastiness, but I'm not that person any more. I made my peace with it a long time ago."

"And it was all my idea," Ann said.

"Are you telling me or asking me?"

THE secret to driving after gin and in the dark was to feel your way forward without drawing any attention, to take it slow, but not too slow. Ann had driven the 53 miles between Jasper and Safford's Falls a thousand times in her life, so there wasn't much reason to worry. The radio nickered quiet jazz and the moist night air bloomed through the windows. Ann had set the glass eye on the tiny shelf above the heater switches. In the cobalt shimmer of the dashboard lights, it softly glowed.

She'd tried calling Stephen to sort it all out, but he'd cut her short.

"You have to deal with this on your own," he said. "I don't have the time for it right now." Before he'd hung up, she thought she'd heard music, laughter, but it may have been her imagination. The conversation with Cindy Pierce had unmoored Ann, and she didn't trust her senses.

Still, Ann knew her way to the old neighborhood in Safford's Falls like a blinkered horse to the barn. She also knew the reputation of the place. The furniture mills had closed down, and all the jobs were gone. There had been arson, robberies, a shooting. Yet as she drove down Crescent toward Highland, at first she saw little evidence of decline. Instead, the ghosts of her life there rose up to meet her: the spot in front of Wendell's Grocery where she and Thelma Vrabec had pledged to be friends for life, the basketball court she had gone to every night one summer in the hopes that Brendan Stokowski might do nothing more than notice her.

She slowed the car even more, putting family names to each house she passed: Fowler, Redmond, Appleby, Olson, Windsor, Bechelli, Prouty, Bell. Even in the dark, she could see it now; a roofline sagging, a car up on blocks in a side yard. She stopped for a moment in front of her old house, the one she had lived in every day of her life until she was nineteen. Even in the dark, it looked abraded; the porch railing had half toppled, one rusty gutter dangled into the overgrown shrubs below the living room picture window. It made her sad—not for the decay of it, but for what she had left behind. This had been home, in an elemental way that their big, beautiful home in Jasper never could or would be. This house, Safford's Falls, wasn't what it once had been, but still. How many of the people she had known and loved, who had known and loved her back, still lived here? The ones who didn't move on to something they thought would be better.

After a few minutes, she moved down the block. The Volvo's headlight lenses, scratched and burred from years on the road, shone weakly down the dark, treelined street. She couldn't see house numbers, so she counted from the corner of Ellis Avenue by memory—Jackson, Fryeburg, Constantino, Coggins. She pulled up to the curb in front and shut off the car.

Ann had always remembered Myra Coggins' house as small and shabby, but it seemed bigger now, even stately, a trim colonial with a wraparound porch and a wide brick chimney rising above. The light from the front porch bled onto the flower stand, a tidy, hand-built shack at the edge of the street. Ann saw hanging tin buckets where cut stems were set to nod, a shelf in front of a broad, open walk-up window, a clappered bell for customers to ring. The scent of lilacs tinted the air; cicadas softly buzzed. The drive had sobered her somewhat, but with that sobriety came a measure of fear.

When Ann had left Jasper earlier in the evening, she'd known exactly what she wanted to do. Now she had no idea. Could she simply stroll up the front walk and knock on the door, glass eye in her hand? What, exactly, was she supposed to say? The house looked warmly lit and welcoming; she saw neatly arranged bookshelves, the shade of a stained glass lamp. But that welcome wasn't for her, hadn't been, for more than two decades, and with good reason.

She had made up her mind to leave, had put the Volvo in gear, when a voice came out of the darkness.

"Can I help you with something?"

Ann strained, but she couldn't make anyone out. Then a woman wearing a cotton summer dress and a canvas apron stepped into the light.

"We usually close at six," the woman said. "But if it's an emergency, I'll do what I can."

"No thanks, I—"

"Ann Marie?" the woman said. "Is that you?"

The last time Ann had seen Deirdre Coggins was in the Cayette County courthouse in 1994. Deirdre, Myra's older, prettier sister, had already gone off to NC State, but had come home for the trial. Back then, Ann had been unable to see anything on the faces of the Coggins family but anger and scorn—if she could look at them at all. But the voice she heard now sounded kind.

"I've seen you come by here," Deirdre said. "More than once. Myra said she'd seen you, too. That was you, wasn't it?"

Ann quickly palmed the glass eye, slipped it into her purse.

"Well," Deirdre said. "Maybe it wasn't. Lots of people drive Volvos these days."

Deirdre leaned down, put her hand on Ann's arm.

"Why don't you come in and have a cup of tea?"

Ann shut off the car and got out, let herself be sleepwalked down the mossy slate path to the Coggins' porch, up the broad wooden steps, along the oriental carpet runner to the door, and inside.

If the exterior of the Coggins house had seemed at odds with Ann's memory, the inside was a museum of her childhood:

the steep oak staircase they had ridden down on folded blankets when she and Myra were only five; the nook in the front hall they'd spent hours curled up in, with tumblers of cherry Kool-Aid and girls' adventure books. The green and white linoleum on the kitchen floor had buckled at the edges in a few spots, but she still remembered how it felt on her bare feet, tiptoeing in for a glass of water in the middle of a hot August day. And the smell—the dry musk of ancient rugs, the sharp, acerbic odor of cedar that wafted in from the hedges, the sweet stink of Mr. Coggins' pipe tobacco, which lingered even now, him gone a decade or more.

As children, she and Myra were inextricably woven into a cozy nest of favorite things, whispered secrets and hideaways, places where the world outside didn't matter, not really. And then, suddenly, it did.

It was the first week of seventh grade, and she, Patty McCauley, and a few other girls had dipped into Tarlow's corner store to get Cokes for the walk home from school. Patty was a frosh, a newly minted cheerleader. She wore lipstick, shopped at the Highland Mall, had let Tommy Winters put his hand on her thigh and keep it there. To Ann, she seemed exotic as a distant planet.

What had Patty McCauley seen in Ann, who until recently, had been only a little girl? Her looks maybe, willowy and blonde, with breasts that had appeared miraculously over the summer, startling her into an uncomfortable awareness that things would not be as they had been. Or maybe it was her weakness.

"You stick with me," Patty had told Ann the day they'd met, "and you'll be in. If you don't, you're doomed."

Huddled at the back of the wood-floored aisles of Tarlow's, the girls had just pulled the cool, sweating bottles from the chest cooler when the bell on top of the door rang and in walked Myra Coggins. Even today, Ann could feel the simple joy of seeing Myra, who'd been away at her grandparents in

Raleigh for the last month of the summer. Ann raised her hand to wave, and Patty McCauley grabbed her wrist and pulled it down, hard.

"For Christ's sake, don't even look at that fucking hippopotamus," Patty said. "She's disgusting." And Ann understood immediately and completely that she had a decision to make.

Myra saw them then; her Chiclet teeth broke a goofy smile.

"Hey, Tootsie Pop," Myra called to Ann, their secret nickname for each other publicly and mortifyingly revealed.

"What the hell are you talking about?" Ann said.

In the alien silence that followed, Myra's eyes filled with tears.

"HERE," Deirdre Coggins said, pointing to the old cherry kitchen table where Ann and Myra had spent scores of nights playing rummy and spoons, before adolescence had ladled out its horrors. "You just sit."

Suddenly, Ann felt wrung out; the last of the gin had burned off, but its effects lingered. She couldn't make her brain work right; she wanted to close her eyes and stop telling the story of her life, but it wasn't yet time.

"She sent me a package," Ann said.

"Oh, Lord. She was completely out of it with the morphine by then. It's a wonder it even got there. I told her not to do it, and she said she wouldn't. I don't know what good she thought it would do."

"No," Ann said. "It's OK. After what I did to her, I deserve it."

Deirdre set two steaming ceramic mugs on the cherry table. She went back to the counter, cut two slices of coffee cake, laid them carefully on china sandwich plates, brought them to the table and sat down. Her face was chubbier than Ann remembered it, but without wrinkles; her eyes a magnificent shade of blue. Ann remembered how she and Myra had envied Deirdre, a woman practically, with eyeliner and padded bras, boys calling at the front porch and cars idling at the curb.

Deirdre sipped her tea.

"It was the cancer she hated, not you. At the worst parts of it, she wanted to hurt somebody who was luckier. That's why she sent that package."

"I don't know why she wouldn't hate me."

"For quite a while," Deirdre said, "she thought she did. It was hard. She was a teenage girl. She knew she wasn't beautiful, but she wanted to at least believe she was pretty. And then she lost her eye, and got that glass thing. The first one, I don't know if you even saw it back then, but it wasn't natural. I could barely stand to look at it, let alone how she must have felt."

Ann told herself she wouldn't cry.

"Here's the thing, though," Deirdre said. "It wasn't the eye. For Mom and Dad, for the lawyers, it was. But not for Myra. For her, it was losing you as a friend. She couldn't understand why you gave up on her like that. And by the time she figured it out, you'd run away to Jasper."

Run away? All her life, Ann had believed she'd chosen a better place. But suddenly, she began to see it all differently. She remembered those months after the accident, the skin-crawling guilt, the desperate adherence to the story, the bewildering terror of the lawsuit. Everywhere she went, the drug store, the schoolyard, the church, the eyes of judgment fell upon her. At the center of her life lay a deep, black gouge, a desperate longing to escape the teenage drama of girls hating girls out of pure unalloyed fear. She'd been a girl once, a little girl, and they'd taken that away from her. She'd wanted nothing more than to be a girl again.

Deirdre nudged the tiny plate toward her. "Do you want some cake? It's up to you."

"Why didn't she call me?"

Deidre's laugh shook the bun of thick yellow hair pinned up on top of her head.

"Why didn't she call you? Come on, Ann. First, the lawyers, then the settlement. And then you left. It wasn't like you moved away. It was like you died."

Suddenly, sickeningly, Ann realized it was exactly that. She had left everything and everyone she had ever loved, to go to the undiscovered country. And none of it had turned out to be better, no matter how much she tried to convince herself. Worse, this was a death that she had chosen—the death of running rather than fighting; the death of living another person's life. She had had done a terrible thing to a friend, and compounded the misery by making an even worse choice. She had chosen under duress, certainly. But the choice had been her own.

"I'm so sorry," Ann said. "I'm so terribly sorry."

Deirdre took her hand.

"Don't be. Myra was a good person. She had a happy life."

"I don't believe in heaven," Ann said. "I don't. I go to church every Sunday, but I think heaven is ridiculous."

"First you were drunk, and now you're morose. There are other options, you know."

"Such as?'

"Such as sleeping. There's a beautiful bed in the guest room, with clean sheets. And this cake will taste just as good in the morning."

Ann thought about Stephen and Angela, how long they could survive without her.

"Can I?" she asked.

"If I didn't want you here, why would I ask? Come on," she said, holding out her hand. "You know where the guest room is. I'll find you an extra toothbrush."

IN the room next to Myra's, Ann found cool cotton sheets, a down pillow, a window to let in cool night air and morning sun. Dierdre came in with a pair of grey cotton pajamas, set a glass of water on the varnished maple nightstand.

"I put that toothbrush on the sink in the upstairs bath-room," she said. "There are towels there, too, if you want a shower. And you sleep as late as you want, Ann. I'm an early riser, but I tend to be quiet."

After Deidre left, Ann slowly undressed and changed into the pajamas, took her purse from where she'd set it in the chair by the door. It took a moment to find it, but the glass eye was still there. She sat on the edge of the bed, held it in her hand until it felt warm and familiar, a part of herself. She pulled back the covers and lay down, switched off the bedside lamp and closed her eyes. Slowly, carefully, she set the curved glass object on top of her left eyelid. Alone in the darkness, she saw everything.

Night Train

On the first floor of the big, gray-shingled rooming house we lived in, Mr. Canfield kept horses. He hired men to come in and knock out the walls of Mrs. Ginoli's long-abandoned dining room, carry in some haybales. When they were done, you wouldn't have known there'd been a table there where hungry oil drillers and lumbermen ate, a kitchen where Mrs. Ginoli cooked for them three times a day. It was a stable, with a bare wood floor and the window frames pulled out like bad teeth, the glass saved and taken away, a big opening cut across the face of it and covered over with a sliding wooden door. And then they brought the horses. That was how the Depression came to Valia, as far as I'm concerned. With five used-up horses in the back of an old truck.

I remember the day the horses came. Leaning on the windowsill of our second-floor apartment, I could see the big, rusty-carcassed truck crawling and pitching down the rutted dirt of the alley, a canvas tarp covering its wooden-slatted cargo box. Spouts of ruddy claydust filled its wake and the roar of its motor ripped the morning quiet. If I had known what the truck and its horses would later mean to me, I would have wept. But I was an eight-year-old boy in the first week of summer vacation. When the truck stopped on the street in front of the rooming house, its shut-down engine hissing and tapping as it lost its heat to the cool air of morning, I pulled on my old leather shoes and ran down to the street.

It hadn't rained for weeks, and dust hung on the air for long after the truck had stopped. Laid-off sawmill and oilfield men, half-drunk already with beer mugs in their weighty paws and no work in sight waded through the dust from the back doors of Scotty's Tap to watch the driver and his helper unload.

The driver was a gigantic man, with a huge red beard growing down his chest and a clot of snuff in his long, crooked jaw. He jumped down from the truck, yelling as he hit the ground. "Drop that ramp down from the top! Let's get these son of a bitches out of here!" His helper unhooked the plank ramp fastened to the back end of the truck laid it out from truckbed to the porch of the rooming house.

The driver pulled open the truck's back gate with a rusty screech and I could see the horses. The five of them huddled together in the slatted wooden box, quivering, nervous, popping their hooves against the truckbed, the light that slid in through the slats of the truck igniting the dust motes the horses stirred.

My whole body thrilled as I watched them; I felt their excitement, felt the small explosions of their calves and flanks, the urgent fear that broadened their nostrils. The smell of them caught the air: ammonia, cut hay, and lather. I breathed in deep and somehow the smell comforted me, as if I had known it my whole life.

Standing behind the truck, the driver gestured to his helper. "Get in there and chase 'em out."

"Chase 'em yourself," the helper said, eyeing the horses. They coiled in the back of the truck box, ears laid back and showing their teeth.

The helper was skinny like the horses were, worked hard and underfed. He had thick, straight black hair and knotty muscles, a greying undershirt pasted to his dark skin with sweat. He stood on the porch of the rooming house and looked down at the men in the street. "Any of you fellas who wants to try can go ahead," he said. "But remember, I seen these nags put in this truck. Far as I'm concerned, they can come out at Christmas."

The driver scowled and spat, yanked a five pound sledgehammer from behind the truckseat. He crawled up onto the hood of the cab, then onto its roof. The horses began to shift and snort, bang up against the slat walls of the truck.

"Holy Jesus," Louie Green said, and spat in the dirt. "He's gonna hammer 'em out."

"Stand clear of that door," the driver said. He pulled back the hammer and slammed it against the front of the wooden box. Terrified, the horses bundled, wheeled, and launched themselves toward daylight and into it, small and grey and black and dun, tangle-maned and scrofulous, kicking holes in the heat. They burst through the doorway into the stable, and the driver's helper slid the door shut behind them and closed the hasp with a wooden peg.

"Ain't you got no lock for that door?" Bill Sims hollered from the street. "Horses as nice as that are sure to get stole."

The men laughed.

"Get up here and get yourself a better view," the driver said, joining the laughter as he climbed down. "From far away, maybe they look ugly as hell. Up close, they got charm."

The men walked over to the porch, moved up to one of the windows. Louie Green lifted me up so I could see. The horses were small and hungry-looking, with clots of dung burred into their tails, scars on their shoulders and flanks. They must have been beat, I thought, wondering what kind of person could do such a thing. I had no experience then with horses, and couldn't imagine them as any kind of trouble.

Once the horses were in the stable, the driver's helper slid the big stable door closed and locked it with a chunky bronze hasp lock. He dropped the key into the front pocket of his coveralls and climbed into the door of the truck. The driver heaved himself up on the other side, pulled his door, and fired up the big motor. As the truck pitched its way back down the alley, the other men wandered back across the dirt street to the back door of the taproom, leaving me and the horses on our own.

About all I did know about horses was that they could be spooked, so I crept up to the stable window slowly and quietly. Eyes rolling to show the whites, the horses shifted nervously, rattled air through their big velvety nostrils. But I saw something else, too, something that wasn't fear. They wondered about me, was all, and that might be the first part of friendship. Already, I imagined how they would learn to stop being afraid, to let me brush their manes and scratch their noses, even swing up onto their backs and ride.

WHEN Poppa came back from his job at Mr. Canfield's oil refinery that afternoon, I was still watching the horses, so I didn't hear him come up behind me.

"Them are the ugliest broncos I ever seen."

His high, cigarette-scraped voice startled me and I jumped a little. Inside the stable, the horses scattered and broke, then as quickly tangled back into a quivering knot. One horse, the dun, lifted his head from the center of the pack and looked dead at me, I was sure.

"No they ain't, Poppa," I said "They're pretty horses, is what I think."

Poppa chuckled. "To a starved coyote," he said. "Maybe." He squatted down, rested his hands on my shoulders and pulled me back against his broad, solid chest. He smelled like oil, tobacco, and sweat, and the hard muscles of his arms surrounded me and pulled me into a hug.

"Son of a gun," he said, his roughwhiskered cheek pressed against my own. "I heard he was gonna bring 'em here, but I didn't believe it. Jesus, they're sorry lookin'." He scrubbed his knuckles on the top of my head. "When did they bring 'em in?"

"This morning."

"And you been here all day."

"Yessir."

"You must be as hungry as I am."

"I ain't. I'd rather watch them horses."

"They'll be here," Poppa said. "At least most of 'em will be. A couple look like they could die of old age any minute." He slung me upside down over his shoulder and stood up.

"Poppa! No. I want to stay here." And when he started walking toward the door, "NO. I ain't hungry. Eat without me."

Poppa carried me up the stairs, toward the smell of fresh bread and fried meat. "I heard he was gonna bring 'em and I couldn't believe it," he said, pausing at the door to shuck off his oily boots, balancing me precariously across his shoulders. "And damned if he didn't."

Momma was at the table when we came in. Poppa swung me down onto the floor. "Momma!" I said.

"I seen 'em."

We washed up in the sink and sat down. The meat went around, and then the bread.

After a few minutes if silence, Momma spoke. "What's he have 'em here for, John?"

"Ask him."

"Somebody else could've kept that dining room goin' after she died. Could've sold all her furniture and let them rooms out. I don't see why. They come and took all that furniture to the dump and burned it."

"Let 'em out to who?" Poppa said. He tined another piece of meat off the platter. "Glass plant's closed. Lumber mill's closed. Most of them men're gone. Nobody to cook for." He smiled. "Besides, if I know Canfield, he's got some way to make a dollar out of them horses. Might be he's just keepin' 'em there for the knackers. They look like glue horses to me."

"Well. If he's gonna get to the slaughterhouse I hope he gets there quick. Horses and humans weren't meant to live in the same place." She lay her fork silently down on her plate and pushed it slowly away, her green eyes flat. "They just weren't meant."

After dinner, Poppa got up from the table and went out on the back porch to smoke. I followed him out.

"They ain't had water," I said. "Can I haul some from Scotty's spigot?"

"Don't get too attached. Cause they ain't yours."

"I won't," I said. "Promise."

The back porch looked down on the railroad track. Further beyond was the slaughterhouse, grey and square on its haunches, butted up against the banks of the deep, green Allegheny. Greasy black smoke rose from its brick stack, and it took on grim shadows in the afternoon light.

"Canfield wouldn't slaughter 'em, would he?"

"He might," Poppa said. "But I wouldn't worry about it. He's probably got some use for 'em, or else he wouldn't have 'em tearing up the downstairs like that."

"Poppa?"

"What?" He threw his cigarette butt down onto the tracks.

"Do you like horses?"

"I do." He turned from the porch railing, his tall, lean body outlined against the blue of the Pennsylvania sky. "I do. But don't try to set me against your mother. Cause she don't like horses. At all."

"Why?"

"Good reasons you and I ain't gonna talk about. Go get 'em some water."

I couldn't lure them close enough to touch. They stood back in the far corner of the stable while I leaned in the window and lowered the bucket to the ground. I cooed and whispered, dipped my hand in the bucket and flung cool enticements toward them. They stood half spooked for ten minutes or more, then they came forward, jostling to the bucket, slapping their tongues against the wet floorboards when it tipped and spilled. While they drank, I moved a bit closer, enough to see the scars. Sprays of them bloomed over haunches, necks, noses like skeletal bouquets. Thin, clean scars that looked like they'd been cut with whips, deep, broad ones high up on the shoulders. I wondered who had hurt them and why they'd done it. "Don't worry," I whispered while they drank. "I won't let nobody else hurt you." They drank like their stomachs were full of dust, and I hauled water until almost sundown.

THAT evening, I sat on the porch and leaned against the wall next to the stable door, listening to the night sounds of Valia. Laughter and the rattling of dishes tumbled across the alley from the back door of Scotty's; a car passed on Main Street, two blocks beyond. In the pothole swamps by the Allegheny, a million peeper frogs shrilled, their song wrapping a warm gauze around the night. I closed my eyes and breathed in the sweet smell of the horses, listened to the gentle rasp of their breathing, the warm shuffle of their hooves against the wooden floor. I lay down on the rough porch boards, the warm drift of horse dung and hay filling up my lungs. Soon I fell asleep.

When I woke, the moon was high in the sky and headed toward morning. The late train sounded at the refinery siding far upriver and came on, its clamor beginning to pile up and push down the valley. From inside the stable came a stuttering of hooves. A kick exploded against the wallboards. I rose and moved to the window. In the back of the stable, at the edges of where the moonlight fell, the horses shifted frantically, stamped and blew.

Rails popped and the ground began to shudder. The horses pitched, stumbled and charged to one end of the stable, crashed to a stop, wheeled and charged back.

When the train sounded at Valia Crossing, the horses

churned into frenzy. The locomotive's headlight lit the stable like a jack o' lantern's hollow, and I knelt at the window enthralled as they rose, kicked, fishtailed and bit, their teeth huge, square, and deathly yellow in the brilliant silver light. They punctured the heavy night air with their forehooves and slammed the walls with their back, screaming, trying to break free.

Their fears of men overridden by terror as the train came on, they passed within inches of me, and in just the moment before the engine passed, swallowing all the noise in the valley and taking it south toward the Pittsburgh steelmills, I reached my hand in through the window and brushed a steaming flank, fell back against the shivering wooden walls as the roaring night moved again toward stillness, cupped my hands before my face and breathed it, this wonderful smell, this smell of horse.

"Walter!" Momma stood at the bottom of the stairwell, leaning out of the doorway, wrapped in her cotton night dress, her long hair falling.

She spoke again as the sound of the train fell away and the horses regained their stillness, as the silence fell on Valia that it lived with every night. "What are you doing out of bed?"

"Nothing." I got up off my knees and moved toward the door, wiping the horse smell on my dungarees.

"You scared me," she said, angry. "I went in your room and you wasn't there. I heard them horses goin' wild and I thought you was killed."

She took me by the elbow and turned me roughly toward the stairs. "Get up them steps. And don't you let me catch you out here past bedtime again. Just don't let me." She caught the back of my head with a rough slap.

Up we went through the dark hallway, Momma herding me in front, past the silence of the Johnson's apartment and the cat-piss stench of the Taylor's. Poppa met us in the kitchen, standing in his undershorts in the light of the overhead bulb.

"He was with them horses, John Ashford," Momma said. "I'll beat his ass like it ain't been beat before if he pulls this again."

"Get to bed," Poppa said. I went to my room and closed the door, curled onto my small mattress and slept, my perfumed hand held before my face, dreaming horse dreams.

THE next afternoon the driver came back alone, his truck empty. He pitched down the rampboard from the top of the truck and lay it out, then tied heavy manila rope to form railings from the stable door to the door of the truck.

"You takin' em?" I said, standing on the porch barefoot in my dungarees. My insides felt like some dead thing.

"That's what I'm doin'." The driver swung open the door of the truck and tied it back, speaking without turning around.

"To the slaughterhouse?" I could barely say the word.

"Hell." he said. "Don't I wish it. I'd kill 'em myself, just to get rid of 'em. But I ain't the kind of person that gets opportunities. I gotta haul 'em every goddam day. Out to the fairground and them turn around and bring 'em back. Mister Canfield's racin' 'em out there. They ain't much, but neither's the competition. Stand back outta the way."

He opened the stable door and ran straight at the horses. "Haw! Get out of here, ya fuckin' nags!" He waved his arms and slapped his thighs, stomped his heavy boots on the hollow wooden floor. The horses panicked and bolted, orbited the hollering driver twice as if they were being whirled on a sling, and shot from the door and into the truck. He ran out behind and closed the truck door, breathing hard through his beard.

"Fuckers are gonna kill me." He lifted the ramp up onto the top of the truck and coiled the heavy manila ropes. I followed him to the cab of the truck, gathered the courage to speak just as he hoisted up into the driver's seat.

"Mister."

He started up the engine, and I climbed up on the running board and pushed my face in through the window. The inside of the cab smelled liked spilled kerosene and beer.

"Mister!" I shouted above the sound of the engine.

"What?"

"I could help with them horses."

"Shit."

"I could."

"Get down off the runnin' board. If I don't get to the fairground by two, same thing'll happen to me as happened to that skinny bastard was with me yesterday."

"But I been waterin' 'em."

"Is that who done it? I come by earlier and it was done already." He pulled his snuff can out of his front pocket and levered a wad into the pouch of his lower lip. "All right. You're hired to water. And shovel out the shit while I'm gone. Pay's a nickel a day. Between you and me, or Canfield'll have my ass. Now get down off that runnin' board."

He put the truck in gear as I jumped to the ground. The truck revved, and trailing a gust of oily smoke, pitched and rolled toward the opposite end of the alley from where it came.

A nickel a day was more than I could believe possible. I saw them already, stacked and shiny, ten weeks of nickels before school started alone. I climbed into the stable through the window, took the shovel out of the corner and shoveled the shit out the back windows into the gully by the railroad track. The fresh, hopeful smell filled me with its promise.

THE summer got hotter and drier. Poppa went to work every day, but I heard him and Momma talk more than once about the refinery. Some people said Canfield was losing money, and that he might close it down. But for every one of those rumors, there was another one—the refinery was doing fine, and Canfield was just trying to scare off a strike. No one knew what the truth was, but Momma worried. For the most part, she kept it to herself, but a small boy could hide in even our tiny apartment, or go unnoticed; more than once, I heard her talking to herself, but couldn't make out the words. When she did speak out, it was never about the refinery, or what it's closing might mean. It was about the horses.

They went wild at every passing night freight and the smell of them rose until it stuck to everything—our clothes and our furniture smelled like horse, our food and our air tasted of it. I lay at night in my room and counted my nickels, reveling in the smell. The sound of the horses when the night trains came only rocked me deeper to sleep. Momma paced her nights away, washed our clothes again and again, grew to dread the trains. One evening in mid-July, she brought it to a head.

"Them horses are driving me mad, John."

"What?" Poppa took another slice of bread and buttered it. I tore the skin off a leg of chicken.

"Them horses," I said. "I haven't slept in a week."

"You'll get used to it."

"I won't." Momma got up from the table and stood looking out the back porch screen. "It ain't the smell I mind so much, John; it's where I'm at when I'm smellin' it. Look at where we are. It ain't nothin' like we talked about years ago. For Christ's sake, John. A horse barn."

"You read the newspapers lately? Lots of people would be glad to be here."

"I ain't one of them people, John. I want them horses gone. I want to be able to sleep nights. You can tell Canfield or I'll tell him."

Daddy just cleared his throat. He knew the same thing

Momma and everybody else in Valia did: Mr. Canfield wasn't anybody to start up with.

Momma came back to the table and sat. She had the same calm she'd have forty years later, dying. "You tell him or I will, John," she said. Her voice was quiet, and I could hear the first evening peepers calling from the potholes beside the river. "I'd rather be put out than live like this. Every time the night train comes. That's more than I can stand."

AFTER supper I went down to haul water. The horses drank greedily, the trail of water dripping from the spigot to the stable quieted the dust. Poppa sat on the steps of the rooming house, smoking a cigarette and watching. It had been weeks now, and the horses came closer than before. "Husssh," I said, reaching my hand into through the window. Clucked my tongue. They came closer, but still out of reach. Poppa crept across the porch and squatted beside me.

"They're almost comin', ain't they?"

"Yep."

"They're tryin' to get over what someone else done to 'em, is all. Same as a person would." He took a nickel out of his pocket. "Run over to Wolcott's Lunch and get an apple. They'll come on."

I ran through the golden evening, the dust thrown from my bare feet, through the alley and across Valia's wide and ramshackle main street, into the bright, antiseptic light of the lunch counter and back through the dust in minutes, an apple in my hand.

We crept to the window and I dangled in a fat Cortland. "There," Poppa whispered, crouching beside me. "Look at that fella's nose open up. He ain't so afraid now, is he?" One of the horses, dung-brown and slatribbed, moved separate from the rest, the first I'd seen one of them move apart.

"Hold your arm still," Poppa whispered. "And watch yourself. It's probably been a long time since he's had an apple. He might not remember they don't have fingers."

Four of the horses stood in the back corner, levered their heads up and down, from side to side, stretched their necks and sniffed, but their feet stayed still. The fifth came slowly closer. "Still," Poppa said. He grabbed my arm and held it steady, and I felt the rough certainty of his hand. The horse shuffled nearer yet. One step. Another.

I felt warm breath on my hand and the apple was gone. The horse skittered back a few steps and stood, grinding his jaw. Poppa wrapped me in his arms and I fell back against his broad chest, felt his heart beating as fast as my own.

We sat on the steps of the rooming house while the sun turned Valia's streets to golden, then plum, while the starlings tucked under the eaves and the swallows came, swathing what remained of the day in buntings of darkness. The lights came on in Scotty's and washed yellow into the alley. The nine o'clock churchbell rang and faded. I sat with Poppa on the porch, my hand glowing where it had been touched, still warm, perhaps, from the horse's breath. Poppa pulled me next to him and stroked my hair.

"Walter," he said, "I'm gonna have to tell Canfield to take them horses away."

"Don't."

"I'd rather have your Momma than them horses." He lit up a cigarette and the match flame played deep shadows on his face. "She don't see the romance in 'em like you and me. To her, they just mean she lives in a horse barn. And she lived in one before. Worse. I promised her no more. You haven't seen life outside of town. How it gets."

I tried to picture Momma as a girl, growing up with a hard life, but all the pictures I could see were beautiful. Then I remembered the horses' scars. Did Momma have those? I pictured them on parts of her I couldn't see.

Poppa stood up. "I'm going' upstairs, Walter. You comin'?"

"Nosir."

"All right," he said. "But when your mother calls, come up straightaway."

After Poppa went upstairs, I sat on the porch listening to the horses snuffling in the dark, nosing for oats. Maybe Momma grew up with someone to take care of her like Canfield took care of his horses, I thought. Maybe she seen the scars on them horses and it was too much to bear.

THE next morning, Poppa left for work as usual, but it wasn't more than a few hours before he came home again. I'd finished cleaning out the stable, and was sitting on the front porch, drinking a glass of water. I saw the glint of Poppa's dinner-bucket clear from the end of the alley. I recognized his long, lopy walk.

I turned and ran to the stairway, yelled for Momma the whole way up. When I came through the door, she was staring out the window, looking down the narrow canyon of the alley. "Hush." she said. "I know."

"He let me go." Poppa put his dinner bucket on the table and unsteadily sat down, drew his oil-clabbered boots up under his chair.

"I went to his office and asked him if he'd take them horses out. 'It ain't right for one man to tell another how to run his business,' he said. By the time I got back to the line, the foreman had wrote my job down as cut back."

Momma sat on Poppa's lap and cried. I watched her across the table. It was the first time my heart ever broke.

"I got a line on some work," Poppa said when she stopped crying.

"There ain't any work," She stood up, spooned some coffee

grinds into a pot and poured water, put it on the stove.

"Stew Stokes told me they're lookin' for welders in Pittsburgh. Said if I get there in time, he's got a cousin can get me on. I can send money back."

"No."

"It's three times what that bastard Canfield pays. I'll get a place and you and Walt can come on later. Leave them horses right here."

"I know women who heard that same story."

"You ain't one of 'em. It's a chance, is all. I'm catchin' onto the train tonight when it stops at the refinery. The loadin' crew'll leave a car open for me. I'll be in Pittsburgh in the morning."

I ran around the table and fell across Poppa's knees. He pulled me up on his lap and held me, rocked me, kissed my forehead, held my hands in his.

"It's my fault," Momma said.

She sat down at the table with a cup of coffee she'd poured, eyes swollen, hair pulled back into a braid.

"It ain't."

I got up from Poppa's lap and went to my room, listened as their low voices filtered through the heat, fading to silence as they closed their door.

THAT night, we said goodbye to Poppa in the dark, dusty alley, both of us crying. He walked to the alley's south end in the whispery slant of moonlight with a canvas bag over his shoulder. Filtered through tears, he looked like a stranger. Poppa turned and waved, then headed down the road toward the refinery siding where he could catch the train.

It was well after midnight. Momma and I waited on the porch of the rooming house for the train to pass. The whistle's moan when it left the refinery siding was the first we heard; it would be moving slowly then, Poppa swinging up into an open boxcar.

"It ain't any good," Momma said when she heard the whistle. "None of it is."

Inside the stable, the horses heard the whistle, too; they shifted and blew and banged the walls with their hardshod feet. We stood at the stable window and watched as they grew wilder, charged and stumbled and screamed. "It's almost here," Mama yelled above the noise of the horses and the oncoming train. She took me by the arm and led me to the stable door. When the freight blew at Valia Crossing, she pulled the wooden peg from the hasp and slid the door wide.

Before she could stop me, I dodged inside.

"Bastards!" I screamed, tasting iron-hard blood in my throat. "Bastards! Haw! Haw! Get out of our house!" The was floor slick with their stench and they roiled around me. I slapped flanks and hollered, waved my arms to drive them out.

After a few cuts around the stable, the horses crashed through the doorway, tumbled in a shrieking pile on the hard dirt floor of the alley and lunged afoot, me and Momma behind, chasing them down the alley back the way they came. Down the alley we ran, the horses well ahead and becoming pale shadows. At the end of the alley I reached in my pocket, pulled out the nickels and threw them after. By the time the coins hit the ground, Poppa was gone.

In His Condition

y Uncle Billy sailed to Formosa in December of 1953, on the merchant freighter *Pamplona*. It is easy for me to imagine him there, even thirty years later, but it is hard to know the way that he lived. I am staying now in a room that he has stayed in, sitting on a bed that he has slept in, but his life, like the island he lived on, is far away. I make him up again and again, from what I know and what I imagine, from the tales my mother told me and the tales she would not, apocryphy upon apocryphy. I make him up from other things. This note he sent me. This butterfly.

I pick up the butterfly's box, run my fingers along the lime colored paperboard, the Chinese characters embossed in silver on its sides. I slowly lift the lid. The insect is sealed between sheets of plastic, its colors those of an aging carnival. Indigo. Magenta. Sunflower. I turn it over in my hands. The stationary is as brittle as the husk of a dead wasp. The lettering is faded, the color of iron, and the note has little to say.

The genus is Danaus. The species is magda. It is native to the Chinese island of Formosa, where it was collected and mounted by myself, William Richard Tamblin, 14 August, 1962. It is my gift to you, Raymond Harrison, on your ninth birthday.

The name Formosa was brought to the island by the Portuguese, a delivery nearly as improbable as my uncle's being delivered there by the *Pamplona*, a merchant vessel shipping machine parts out of New Orleans. I picture sallow-colored fishermen trying to draw this lush new word, this Formosa, across lips stung with salt and wind. I picture Uncle Billy, a canvas duffel over his shoulder, his long, spider-jointed legs spindling down the gangplank to the wharf, where the punctual, foreign shouts of the men who hauled on the crates and cables, who bought and sold beef and detergent and fuel oil and fish, were welcome, a proof that his abandonment of America was complete.

I am in the house of my childhood again, in the bedroom I slept in then. The room is redolent with memories of bat crack and mitt leather, memories made tragic by the way I have abandoned my life. I am here because I have nowhere else to go. I could not leave America if I tried.

For seven months now, I have been drunk—on hard liquor mostly, or anything I could get. This is my first morning sober. On the Princess phone in the downstairs kitchen, my mother is talking to doctors, talking to support groups and therapists and dry-out farms. At seventy–two years old, she should not have to care for me, but she does. I listen as her voice struggles up the stairwell, the color of widow's weeds, near exhausted. Sunlight comes through the window at the eastern end of the long, narrow bedroom, seeking the lowest of places. I lean over the edge of the bed and watch it settle onto the floor.

Uncle Billy visited this house once, in December, 1953, eight months after I was born. He was on the run then, I imagine; he was sick, coming to the shelter of the only family he had. A black-and-white photograph taken by my father with a Kodak camera shows Billy against the backdrop of the picket fence in our front yard, holding me at arm's length, his expression solemn, the brilliance of the sun-reflected snow threatening to bleach us both from existence. My uncle looks an unprepared adventurer—skinny, wattle-necked and unshaven, only a pork-pie hat and a thin polyester suitcoat against the cold. His nose is hooked and dangles impossibly far below his upper lip. His teeth have rotten-looking gaps between them and are turned at odd angles.

"He was always distant, even when he lived in this country," my mother says whenever we look at this photograph, then adds with a laugh, as if to comfort herself, "He was distant before he was distant. And you, Raymond, are distant, too. Same as your uncle. There's no doubt about it." When she says this, she means it kindly, in the way all mothers see their children as peculiar and special, but it pains me to the bone.

From the stairwell, I hear my mother patiently cradle the telephone receiver, the rattle as she lifts it to dial again. She knows the best facilities from the worst now, has connections who might find a place to put me before I get thirsty and leave again. She knows this game of time and circumstance. I will only listen to reason for the short time that I am weak enough to hear. She will feed me, give me a place to sleep and nurse me through withdrawal as best she can, but as I get better, I will get worse. I'll find the strength to drink again.

My mother takes her time and tries for a good place, despite the fact that I've told her how little it matters. A detox is just a place to store me. No matter where I go, I will try hard to take the cure or I will not, and the atmosphere will be saturant with what I will not say. What I will not say in detox is this: *I lasted 114 days, and then I took a drink.* What I will not say is this: *You have no answer I have not already heard.* The plastic-sealed butterfly rests on the dingy cotton coverlet. I pick the insect up, turn it over, seeking divination in its tender architecture.

I have made up stories about Billy's voyage, casting him as a romantic sailing toward paradise, but none of these stories are true. My uncle was led to Formosa not by curiosity or adventure, but by want. Formosa was something that I might have done. It was dependency and recklessness, bad timing and desperation. "In his condition," my mother tells me, "he probably had no choice."

Uncle Billy's want was morphine. He got it in World War Two. With glass syringes and liquid the color of a butterfly's wing, the doctors replaced the pain of shrapnel wounds with numbness, and Billy found the numbness irreplaceable. He traveled a lot to keep himself numb—Nashville and New Orleans, Dallas and Key West—taking what he could get, I imagine, any way he could get it.

A week after Billy left our house, clear-eyed, low-voiced men in suits came looking for him, unsure, even, of his real name. They showed badges to my father. "Hong Kong," he told them, and did not lie. "I think he has a flight." Years later when I was in my first detox, my father used this story as a way of explaining how hard it was to have sent me there. "I would have told them where he was going, even without the badges," he said, sitting in a folding chair in the television room, his hands resting formally on his knees. "I loved your Uncle like he was a brother of my own." This explanation meant nothing to me then, but now, when I am sober, I understand.

The indignities that led Billy to end up on the *Pamplona* instead of a plane to Hong Kong, I can only imagine, but the images come with dreadful ease. When you need the numbness badly enough there is no method of providing it that does not involve indignity. I have given my money and my family, my clothing and my sex so that I could be numb. Billy gave up Hong Kong and took Formosa, and if there was a numbness in between then he probably thought fair trade.

Most of Billy's story I am content to imagine, but there is a part of the truth that I need. On the island of Formosa, my uncle was able to extinguish his want. Perhaps it was willpower, ceremony, the relief of escape. Perhaps it was some herb or powder that came in at the docks and was sold at the market stalls in sleeves of butcher paper. Perhaps it was something complicated, perhaps something simple. Perhaps this simple: Collect butterflies.

Danaus magda. I lie back on the forgiving mattress and rub the butterfly between my fingers like medicine. Formosa.

Danaus magda. My salty tongue makes the words again and again, trying to render my want powerless. *Danaus magda. Formosa.* I make this my mantra, this evidence of hope. I imagine Billy finding something that possessed him so fully that he did not want to be numb, but alive.

There are things you grasp at when you cannot have what you need. My mother is playing solitaire now, waiting for a return call. I can hear the cards snapping against the enameled steel of the kitchen table. If I go to the detox, I will play lots of cards. I will use coffee and cigarettes and small talk to try and hold back the want; I will use bravado and humor. I will use the tools that the therapists give us, and know that the tools are inadequate. I will keep looking for something that someone in this condition can really use.

My Uncle Billy died a month ago, still safe on his island. I could not be found for the funeral. My mother told me about it this morning, sitting for a moment on the bed that he slept in, holding my hand as if I were a small child, the flat metal of her hair and the blueness of her wrists crying age. My Uncle Billy died a month ago, his veins healthy and clean. His butterflies—thousands of them, carefully mounted and labeled—were what he left behind.

I do not notice the telephone's ring; I hear my mother's voice of a sudden. It sighs relief, and the receiver cradles down. I have a place to go, and people to be with. We will be scared there, all of us. We will be defiant there, some of us. We will make ourselves up, again and again, from the stories that we tell and the stories we do not tell, apocryphy upon apocryphy. We will look for something, anything, some simple addiction to draw us away.

There are things that you grasp at when you cannot have what you need, and one of these things might save you. I am praying for Billy now, in the room that he has stayed in. I am praying for myself, hoping that I, too, can find some small, saving thing. I am forming the mantra that renders want powerless, turning a butterfly over in my hands.

Certain Miracles

The gas station huddled at the bottom of the hill, back against a wall of snow and pine, a pale yellow rectangle of light leaking from its tiny front door into the West Virginia dark. Becker pushed his sneaker against the brake pedal full force, but overshot the pulloff by ten yards or better. He dropped the LTD in reverse, cranked the wheel on the heel of one hand, and swung backward up to the pump. The big engine made a half–turn and shuddered to a stop.

"Piece of shit," he said. The lit end of his Marlboro waggled in the dark.

He fiddled with the rearview, angled it until he could look down into the back seat. Rose lay curled up next to the driver's side door, underneath an old cotton blanket, softly breathing. It amazed him sometimes how hard she slept, like a little girl would, although she was nearly eighteen and pregnant with a child herself. Every time she woke, it was like she'd died and come back. Certain miracles had kept him from leaving her, and this was one, the way she slept and woke. But those miracles were a problem he needed to get over. He was trying to get south, and she was slowing him down.

Becker unfolded his scrawny body from the LTD's grimy cockpit and slammed the door closed. The rusted–out sidepanel rattled. Cold wind shot through the thin fabric of his Levi jacket and flannel shirt. He shuddered, and his muscles tightened down hard on the bone. The door of the gas station opened. An old man toddled out, dressed in overalls, a dirty wool jacket and cap, gumsoled arctics on his feet.

"Get 'er yourself?" the man asked. His voice came high

and clear and his arctics squeaked in the hard-froze snow as he balanced against the wind.

Becker nodded.

"Thanks. Pay inside." The old man toddled back into the station, pulling the door closed behind himself like some animal covering a denhole.

The pump was timeworn and fussy, but the black and white numbers turned upwards just the same. Becker shut off the pump and holstered its nozzle. He hooked his wallet out of the back pocket of his jeans and poked through it. They had forty-eight in bills, and a jar on the floor of the LTD with another fifteen or so in change. They could get to Lauderdale on that, barely. Once they got there, Carrier would have to put them up. It would be a lot easier without her. Things wouldn't be near so tight.

"Dennis?" Rose climbed out of the car, wrapped in an old Army blanket, her blond hair hung in a sleepy drape about her shoulders, her face pale as the fresh snow banked at the foot of the gas pump. One cheek was creased scarlet where it had pressed against the vinyl seat while she slept.

"Dennis? Is there a bathroom here? I gotta pee."

"You always gotta pee."

"It ain't my fault," she said. "Try bein' pregnant sometime."

He turned and walked toward the station door.

A hand–welded box woodstove squatted in the back corner of the room, and the old man had it heated up good. He sat at a fold-leg card table beside the woodstove working a jigsaw puzzle, stripped down to his undershirt and a pair of green mechanics' overalls, the suspenders unhooked and trailing the floor. He looked up from his puzzle and pointed at Rose, made a motion like wrapping himself in a blanket.

"We don't get many Injuns in here. Did you come by canoe?" His teeth showed briefly, then hid.

"You got a restroom?" She said it 'ristroom,' like someone off a farm.

The old man pointed toward a painted door at the back. "The tank's busted. They's a bucket you can fill at the spigot to flush with."

"Thank you," she said. She went into the bathroom and closed the door.

The old man got up from his table and walked to the cash register, his withered arms held out from his sides like vestigial wings. He looked out at the LTD. "Be about eighteen dollars, I figure."

"Seventeen eighty-five," Becker said. "How'd you know it was empty?"

The old man held out his waxy hand for the bills. "No offense or nothin'," he said, "but you jest look the type."

"You don't know half of it." He turned toward the bathroom. "You comin' out of there today?"

It pissed him off that he was always waiting for her, baby or no baby. The sooner they got to Lauderdale, the better off they'd be. There'd be no more counting pennies in glass jars, no more hundred-dollar cars. He'd seen the 1978 Mustangs, just out in the showrooms. If Carrier was right, he could get himself one.

"I can get you on the Stark Brothers show the whole way across the Sunbelt," Carrier had said on the phone. "You won't see a fuckin' snowflake all winter. Run the Ferris wheel maybe, or the Zipper. Two hundred a week. Maybe triple that, if we partner up."

"Partner up?"

"I'm peddlin' a little dope."

The dealing was another problem. Here it was his first chance to make decent money after nine months of picking apples and digging ditch, and he couldn't even tell her about it. He'd thought about getting her set up in an apartment and taking off, sending her money to cover the bills. That'd be the decent thing. But as the time to the baby got closer, he'd begun to consider other, easier, options.

Becker looked at the LTD. "She's liable to take an hour in there," he said to the old man.

The old man poked at a puzzle piece, turned it around in his hands.

There wasn't a law against leaving. Becker could get in the car right now, eat a handful of speeders, and be in Lauderdale in less than a day. Rose could go back to her mother's, whether her mother liked having a knocked up daughter or not.

He'd half made up his mind when he heard her in the bathroom, singing softly to herself as she washed.

"She's got a nice voice," the old man said. Goosebumps raised on Becker's arm.

The singing was another miracle. After Rose discovered she was pregnant, this music came. She pulled wordless tones out of the air, soft and calming half–melodies that reminded Becker of the songs his mother used to sing when he was a boy. Rose sang because she had a baby in her belly. His baby. He stopped halfway to the door.

BECKER used the bathroom next, and when he came out she stood by the card table. The old man was animated now, his teeth slid out full time. Rose smiled too, her face full and opened up, and it shocked him to remember how pretty was. He stood there for a few seconds, watching.

"I like Ann," she said to the old man, "for a girl. That's my mother's name. Dennis says we ought to call a boy Houdini, because he escaped from the rubber." She laughed.

Becker cleared his throat. "Can you sell me a carton of Marlboros?"

"Ten dollars even," the old man said. He got up from the

table and rattled a keychain that hung on his belt, sorted out the key and opened the cigarette machine. He counted out ten red–and–white packages.

Becker reluctantly tugged a ten out of his wallet. There wasn't a reason to pay. They were out in the middle of nowhere and the machine and the cash register were both open. One tap on the old man's head and their money problems were over. When the old man bent to put the ten in the register, Becker touched Rose's wrist and tipped his head toward the cash drawer.

"No, Dennis." She said it quiet, but loud enough for the old man to hear. He slid open a drawer underneath the register to show a pouch of Red Man chewing tobacco and an elderly six–shot revolver. Becker smiled.

The wind still blew hard, but the old man followed them outside in his tee shirt and stood, yellow and rickety in the snow and false light, the revolver in his hand. "Some men ain't fit to be fathers," he said to Rose as Becker started the LTD. "Get clear of him if you can."

THEY were on the highway now, sixty miles north of Charleston. Becker fiddled with the radio, trying to coax a decent station out of the night. The road was clear of snow and patched white with spent salt, and the LTD was making a steady seventy, scouring dark and trailing darkness as it carried them south. He wondered when they would get below the snow line.

"Eighty-five yesterday," Carrier had said when Becker called him in Lauderdale the day before they left. "Been like that right through. I'm tellin' you, I'm on the beach every day. Get your ass down here while there's still some pussy left that I ain't got."

The thing Becker should have done was not to mention Rose at all. He should have just showed up, made up a story when they got there and there was nothing Carrier could do. Instead, he told the truth, or most of it. Carrier balked.

"Shit, Dennis. How the hell did you get messed up in that? Where we gonna put her, and a kid besides? Them carny trailers are tiny." And then there was silence for a minute, and Becker knew what was coming next.

"Will she sell it, do you think? A good whore could make us big money, Dennis. Better'n dope, and twice as safe."

"Kill me first," Becker said. "Come on, Randy. I'll set her up somewhere down there as soon as I can. Then you and me can take off. Her uncle's a clerk at the courthouse, is all. They'd have me for support."

"My ass," Carrier said. "You're in love with her."

"Doubtful."

"Well, you think about it before you drag her down here. Somethin' like that puts a serious damper on what I'm talkin' about, which is unlimited good times and big fuckin' dollars."

"She's havin' my kid and I'm not gonna leave her," Becker said. After he hung up, he sat alone in the kitchen of his aunt's house trailer for a long time, smoking cigarettes and wondering if what he'd said was true.

THE night had no moon and the highway was nearly empty. They passed a little town in the dark, just a soft white glow of light in the valley below.

"Look at that place," Becker said. "Probably not one person in ten gets out of it. And all it takes is a little guts and a car."

Rose took out a pack of Marlboros and lit one up. "You scared me with that old man at the fillin' station," she said.

"Shit."

"No. I mean it. I know you, Dennis Becker."

"You think he was right, then?"

"About what?"

"That you ought to get clear of me."

She looked at him across the bench seat, lay her hands across her belly. "You're gonna be a father to this child," she said. "If I have to hunt you down."

Becker shook a joint out of his Marlboro pack and lit it up. He took a deep hit and passed it to her across the wide bench seat.

"I'm gonna have your baby, Dennis Becker," she said. "Yours." She hit the joint and a seed popped like a tiny firework in the dark.

"You think it'll look like me," Becker said. He remembered the pictures of himself as a boy, with a felt cowboy hat and a plastic holster and gun at his hip. That would be something, a boy. Or even a girl. Either one would be something to care about. He reached across the seat and pulled Rose close to him, kissed her on the ear.

JUST after eleven they swung into Charleston, West Virginia on the tail end of a freezing rain. The reflections from fast–food signs puddled like lacquers on the wet pavement, and strings of drearily winking lights swung between the lampposts. Becker sidled the LTD up to the curb. The sight of the streetlights put an itch under his nose.

"I'm hungry," Rose said. "Let's hit the Burger King."

"There's bread and there's peanut butter. Make a sandwich. We got to go easy on money."

"More'n half of that money's mine," she said, but he pretended he didn't hear. Somewhere close there must be a bar room. He looked at himself in the rearview mirror, turned off the ignition and opened the door.

"You ain't leavin' me," she said.

He shut the door. She cranked down the window and stuck her head out, blinked back the rain.

"Where are you goin', then."

"Just stay in the god damn car."

"What if I have the baby."

"Find a pay phone. It don't cost anything to call the ambulance. If you're not here when I get back, I'll find you."

She waited a few seconds before she answered back. "You better look for the bus station," she said, "Because that's where I'm headed."

"Promises, promises."

Behind him, Becker heard the LTD window squeak shut. He widened his nostrils like a hound on trail and strode down the main drag, the rain at his face like most every rain he could remember.

SIX blocks or so from the LTD, he found The Coal Tipple Tap, a dirty little factory beer joint with a bar and pool table and dim–lit booths in the back. The place was lively, with the three to eleven shift just come in, big, flannel–shirted millhands with black tin lunchboxes and wads of bills laid up on the counter and Iron City on draft. Becker situated himself at the end of the bar, where he could stay out of trouble and keep an eye on the barmaid.

The millhands had a drink or two and headed home, and by 12:30 the place was almost empty. The barmaid came and put a chair up on her side of the bar and they talked. Her name was Christine and she tended bar every night but Tuesday. She had a will to travel and a body like a house afire.

"I been in Charleston West Virginia twenty-four years, and that's twenty–four years too many," she said. She poked her straw at the ice cubes in her rum and coke. "At the end of the shift I'm leavin'. The car's packed."

"You interested in a companion?" Just the smell of her perfume and the shape of her mouth had him hard.

"No thank you," Christine said. "I had enough shit from men to last me about six lifetimes. The latest left half an hour before you got here. I need a little bit of a break. But I'm not leavin' for another hour and a half. We might have time to say goodbye."

By the time she made the last call, Becker was behind the bar with her, a water glass full of Jack Daniel's in one hand and the other up the back of her skirt. This was more his style. Spur of the moment. She'd be good for the trip south, maybe a couple of weeks after they got there. Then when it came time to hit the Stark Brothers show, he'd be done with her, and go sniffing somewhere else. That was how it usually worked out.

Becker wasn't sure why Rose had happened different. Maybe it was because he'd just got out of the lockup and hadn't had any for six months. Maybe it was that picking seventy-cent flats of strawberries all day in the sun made your brain go bad. Maybe it was the miracle of how it all happened. One minute there was nobody in that hot, dusty field but himself and a bunch of other shitkickers, stooped over and suffering. The next he was in the tall grass by Oswayo Creek kissing the back of Rose' Cameron's bare neck, with heaven pressed between his cock and the curve of her ass, wondering if he'd been driven delirious by the heat.

At first they were crazy for it. She used to push him over on the old couch on the back porch of her grandmother's house and get right on him like a jumper cable was holding her on. He got so he could smell her pussy across the room. Then came the baby, and the scents she gave of were different, warm rather than hot, soft and milky. She felt more like mothering him, she said, less like wanting to fuck.

"I've fucked plenty," Rose said. "Being a mother is something I haven't done."

The barmaid put the last of the drunk rednecks out and turned out the lights.

"You come over here," she said, climbing into a booth.

It had been a month or better since Rose had given him any, and he crawled into the booth and met her tongue with his. Just then, the boy came out from the back room.

"Mom," he said. "When are we gonna leave?" He was six years old or so, with a little pot belly under his dirty tee shirt and his hair shaved down tight to his scalp. He looked at Becker for only a second, as if this was a normal thing. Becker jumped back out of the booth and stood up.

"Timmy Robbins, you get back there and wait for me like I told you, or I'll beat your ass."

"Trisha says she wants to stay with Daddy."

"He ain't your daddy no more. He left. And he wasn't hers to begin with. This here—" she pointed to Becker— "Is Denny. He's gonna be your daddy from now on."

"You are?" The boys eyes shifted uncertainly between his mother and this new man.

Becker took a step back.

"Son of a bitch," the barmaid said." I should've known." Her hands shook as she lit a cigarette. The boy skittered into the back room and his sister yelled out from the dark.

"I am leaving, mother. I am going back to John David's house right now."

Becker turned and pitched toward the bar room door.

HE ran most of the way to the LTD, but when he got there, she was gone. He kicked out one of the taillights and sat down on the curb. A minute later she came out of the alley on the other side of the street, wrapped in the blanket and shivering.

"I got scared," she said. "These fuckers come and hammered on the windows while I was sleeping. They left, but I was afraid they'd come back." She coughed and started to cry.

He took her in his arms and whispered in her ear, like a mother talking to a child, until she quit sobbing. He breathed deeply, smelling her milkiness and the salt in her tears. As they stood in the rain in the dark, empty street, the traffic light down the block buzzed and turned green.

"We gotta get goin', honey," Becker said, and pulled her toward the car, but she stopped him.

"I can't go anywhere now," she said. She smiled, and the world swung on a tilt.

"MOTHER'S information?" The nurse didn't bother to look up. Her voice struggled through the gap at the bottom of the glass partition as if she lacked for air.

Becker bent to the glass and spoke. "Rose Marie Cameron. Born September 26, 1961. Olean, New York. I don't know the ZIP."

The liquor was finally trailing out of his system. The fluorescent light and the disinfectant smell made him sick to his stomach. Rose had labored fourteen hours and had a girl.

"Father's name?"

He paused and let out a breath, weighing his last chance at denial. "Dennis James Becker. Five, thirteen, fifty-nine. Birthplace unknown."

"Congratulations, Mister. You won the prize." The nurse pulled a copy of the birth certificate off the typewriter roller and slid it under the glass.

An orderly came and led him to an elevator. "How's she doin'?" Becker said.

The orderly chuckled. "She looks a helluva lot better than you do."

"Big surprise there," Becker said. "She looked a hell of a lot better'n me to start with."

AN empty, smokestained waiting room looked five floors down onto the parking lot, and Becker could see the LTD, docked close up to the chain link fence at the back of the lot. He pressed his hand against the front pocket of his pants and felt the hard knot of keys there, felt the metal in them pulling toward southern points of the compass. He pulled out a Marlboro and lit it, put his foot up on the windowsill. Further away, back up against the mountains, he saw the tops of eighteen wheelers as they slid along the highway. He wondered what he ought to do, and there wasn't any doubt about it. He damn well ought to hit for Lauderdale.

The orderly tapped his knuckles on the doorframe and Becker turned around. "Y'all wanta see 'em, they're ready."

"They? Oh. Yeah." Becker's heartbeat came up and pushed at the inside of his ear.

He'd never seen a cleaner room in his life. They'd made him wash his hands and face and put on a scrub gown, but he still smelled like road stink, and Rose and their baby lay on the perfect white sheets, washed clean and beautiful, Rose with her hair plaited, the baby asleep on her chest.

"Hi." His voice felt unsure about leaving his throat.

She nodded at the orderly. "Can you hand her over to her daddy?"

The orderly stepped to the bed, gently levered his hands under the baby and lifted. She fussed awake but didn't squall. He showed Becker through pantomime how he was supposed to hold her and passed her over to his hands.

She was lighter than a peck of apples, lighter than a flat of strawberries, lighter than anything he'd ever held. When she stretched against him, he thought she would rise up into the air and levitate above his palms.

"Hey, Annie." Becker smiled. "How about a kiss for your daddy?"

He lifted her up and kissed her on the forehead, and the perfect, freshly-living smell of her washed over him. Her face held the scent deeply and he touched it gently it against his own, breathing long and slow. Every hard muscle in his body relaxed, and then he was crying. He held her there, her small, warm breath blooming in his ear.

IN the waiting room again, Becker smoked a pack of cigarettes, drank half a dozen cups of vending machine coffee. There wasn't a way he could think of to take a baby on the road with the Stark Brothers. That meant the same thing in Florida he'd had in Pennsylvania. Shit work for shit wages. And besides that, being even more tied down. He'd tried to tell Rose it wouldn't work, but she just refused to listen.

"Stay up here and wait," he'd told her. "The carnival comes north in June."

"Bullshit, Dennis Becker. Wait where? My mother won't even talk to me on account of it and my grandma says I gotta be out by the end of the month. I don't have but one place in the world I can go."

If Carrier could loan him some money up front for a place until they turned over some herb, things might work out, but other than that, Becker didn't know. As far as it went, though, Rose and Annie were the only family he had, and he ought to just love them. He ought to stick around. But he felt like a fox near a bait set, smelling steel. Deep inside him was a feeling that told him to run.

Sometime in the early evening, he went to the room to see them. The baby lay in a crib next to the bed, and Rose half–slept, watching. Becker stood in the doorway, whispered.

"Hey, Sweetheart."

Rose smiled and stretched, her eyes full and glossy in the dusk.

"I just wanted to have a peek at her. I didn't want to wake you up." He tiptoed over the crib and knelt beside it watching, lowered a hand inside. Against the rough hide of his knuckles, her skin felt like cream, its heat startling and magnetic, and he stroked her again and again.

"Look at her," he said, and fell into silence.

"I called my sister," Rose said. "Mom said she wants to see her. Can you believe that?"

"How drunk was she?"

"Oh, come on. You know she's quit." She hesitated a second. "We could go back, you know. I mean I understand about you and Randy and Florida and all. But that was before I seen Annie. She's a lot, Dennis."

"She sure is." He smiled, watching the baby's tiny chest rise as fall as she breathed.

"Goin' back to a place where we could stay for nothing and have someone to help out,—that might make things a lot easier," Rose said.

Becker stood up. he walked to the bed and kissed Rose on the cheek. "You need your rest, Mama," he said. "Why don't we just sleep on that one." On his way out of the room, he switched off the lights.

BECKER took the back stairwell out to the parking lot, crawled in behind the wheel of the LTD and spun up a joint, looking up at the rows of windows, warmly lit against the night. He pushed the cigarette lighter in and waited, lit the joint and took one good, deep hit and then another. When he was good and high, he leaned back on the seat and fished his pocket for the keys.

The LTD taxied slowly out to the front of the lot and turned right, toward the highway. For half a block, he watched in the rearview mirror, and from then on he gazed forward. He switched the radio on, found a station, and turned it up loud. It was country music, but Becker didn't care. Any kind of noise could keep the sound of a baby's breathing out of your ear.

Halfway to the North Carolina border, he stopped and picked up a six pack and rolled all the windows down, found an AM station that played good rock and roll, and ate a handful of speed. It was fifteen hours straight through and Carrier would be ready to party. Becker remembered the way good coke felt dripping down the back of his throat.

He crossed the border to nothing—just the road and the dark and the warm, humid air, the tractor trailers ghosting past him in the night. Most of the six pack was gone. He'd burned two joints and was screaming along with Aerosmith on the radio, hammering the dashboard in the best time he could keep. Then the radio quit and he was hammering and screaming alone. He smacked the steering wheel with the heel of his hand, throttled the LTD down and pulled it onto the berm.

There was no flashlight in the car, so he opened the passenger side door and worked by the overhead light. The radio wires all looked good. He opened the fuse box and pulled them one by one, testing. And then he sat for a while, listening to the way the spring wind moved through the trees, feeling it against his skin.

He pulled the Marlboro pack out of his pocket, shook out a cigarette, and propped it in his lip, rummaged for a book of matches. The first match blew out so he tossed it, cupped a second in his hands and held it up to his face. And then he shook the match out and dropped it, pitched the cigarette out the window into the dark.

This was a certain miracle. Even through the sweat and dope, the speed and alcohol and the hours on the road, the sweet, living scent of his daughter clung to him. Becker got out of the car and crossed the highway, found himself a place to sit on the soft new grass of the median strip, a place where he could listen to the spring peepers and taste the night air. He sat there for a long time with his hands cupped under his nose, watching the taillights of the trucks wink into the south, breathing the smell of her until he was full.

About the Author

GARY LEE MILLER learned to tell stories in the bar rooms of northern Pennsylvania and at Vermont College of Fine Arts, where he earned his MFA. His work has appeared in a number of literary magazines, including *Florida Review, Green Mountains Review, Hunger Mountain*, and *Chicago Quarterly Review*. Gary's music writing can be found in *Seven Days*, Vermont's weekly source for arts, culture, and politics. He sings and plays guitar in The TrailerBlazers, a strictly hillbilly outfit. For more information about Gary and his work, please visit garyleemiller.com

Photo — Carley Stevens-McLaughlin

Fomite
Burlington, VT

A fomite is a medium capable of transmitting infectious organisms from one individual to another.

"The activity of art is based on the capacity of people to be infected by the feelings of others."
Tolstoy, *What Is Art?*

Flight and Other Stories - Jay Boyer
In *Flight and Other Stories,* we're with the fattest woman on earth as she draws her last breaths and her soul ascends toward its final reward. We meet a divorcee who can fly with no more effort than flapping her arms. We follow a middle-aged butler whose love affair with a young woman leads him first to the mysteries of bondage and then to the pleasures of malice. Story by story, we set foot into worlds so strange as to seem all but surreal, yet everything feels familiar, each moment rings true. And that's when we recognize we're in the hands of one of America's truly original talents.

Loisaida - Dan Chodorokoff
Catherine, a young anarchist estranged from her parents and squatting in an abandoned building on New York's Lower East Side, is fighting with her boyfriend and conflicted about her work on an underground newspaper. After learning of a developer's plans to demolish a community garden, Catherine builds an alliance with a group of Puerto Rican community activists. Together they confront the confluence of politics, money, and real estate that rule Manhattan. All the while she learns important lessons from her great-grandmother's life in the Yiddish anarchist movement that flourished on the Lower East Side at the turn of the century. In this coming-of-age story, family saga, and tale of urban politics, Dan Chodorkoff explores the "principle of hope" and examines how memory and imagination inform social change.

Improvisational Arguments - Anna Faktorovich
Improvisational Arguments is written in free verse to capture the essence of modern problems and triumphs. The poems clearly relate short, frequently humorous, and occasionally tragic stories about travels to exotic and unusual places, fantastic realms, abnormal jobs, artistic innovations, political objections, and misadventures with love.

Carts and Other Stories - Zdravka Evtimova
Roots and wings are the key words that best describe the short story collection *Carts and Other Stories,* by Zdravka Evtimova. The book is emotionally multilayered and memorable because of its internal power, vitality and ability to touch both your heart and your mind. Within its pages, the reader discovers new perspectives and true wealth, and learns to see the world with different eyes. The collection lives on the borders of different cultures. *Carts and Other Stories* will take the reader to wild and powerful Bulgarian mountains, to silver rains in Brussels, to German quiet winter streets, and to wind-bitten crags in Afghanistan.
This book lives for those seeking to discover the beauty of the world around them, and will have them appreciating what they have—and perhaps what they have lost as well.

Fomite
Burlington, VT

Zinsky the Obscure - Ilan Mochari

"If your childhood is brutal, your adulthood becomes a daily attempt to recover: a quest for ecstasy and stability in recompense for their early absence." So states the 30-year-old Ariel Zinsky, whose bachelor-like lifestyle belies the torturous youth he is still coming to grips with. As a boy, he struggles with the beatings themselves; as a grownup, he struggles with the world's indifference to them. *Zinsky the Obscure* is his life story, a humorous chronicle of his search for a redemptive ecstasy through sex, an entrepreneurial sports obsession, and finally, the cathartic exercise of writing it all down. Fervently recounting both the comic delights and the frightening horrors of a life in which he feels—always—that he is not like all the rest, Zinsky survives the worst and relishes the best with idiosyncratic style, as his heartbreak turns into self-awareness and his suicidal ideation into self-regard. A vivid evocation of the all-consuming nature of lust and ambition—and the forces that drive them.

Kasper Planet: Comix and Tragix - Peter Schumann

The British call him Punch; the Italians, Pulchinella; the Russians, Petruchka; the Native Americans, Coyote. These are the figures we may know. But every culture that worships authority will breed a Punch-like, anti-authoritarian resister. Yin and yang—it has to happen. The Germans call him Kasper. Truth-telling and serious pranking are dangerous professions when going up against power. Bradley Manning sits naked in solitary; Julian Assange is pursued by Interpol, Obama's Department of Justice, and Amazon.com. But—in contrast to merely human faces—masks and theater can often slip through the bars. Consider our American Kaspers: Charlie Chaplin, Woody Guthrie, Abby Hoffman, the Yes Men—theater people all, utilizing various forms to seed critique. Their profiles and tactics have evolved along with those of their enemies. Who are the bad guys that call forth the Kaspers? Over the last half century, with his Bread & Puppet Theater, Peter Schumann has been tireless in naming them, excoriating them with Kasperdom....*from Marc Estrin's Foreword to Planet Kasper*

The Co-Conspirator's Tale - Ron Jacobs

There's a place where love and mistrust are never at peace; where duplicity and deceit are the universal currency. *The Co-Conspirator's Tale* takes place within this nebulous firmament. There are crimes committed by the police in the name of the law. Excess in the name of revolution. The combination leaves death in its wake and the survivors struggling to find justice in a San Francisco Bay Area noir by the author of the underground classic *The Way the Wind Blew: A History of the Weather Underground* and the novel *Short Order Frame Up*.

All the Sinners Saints - Ron Jacobs

A young draftee named Victor Willard goes AWOL in Germany after an altercation with a commanding officer. Porgy is an African-American GI involved with the international Black Panthers and German radicals. Victor and a female radical named Ana fall in love. They move into Ana's room in a squatted building near the US base in Frankfurt. The international campaign to free Black revolutionary Angela Davis is coming to Frankfurt. Porgy and Ana are key organizers and Victor spends his days and nights selling and smoking hashish, while becoming addicted to heroin. Police and narcotics agents are keeping tabs on them all. Politics, love, and drugs. Truths, lies, and rock and roll. *All the Sinners Saints* is a story of people seeking redemption in a world awash in sin.

Fomite

Burlington, VT

Short Order Frame Up - Ron Jacobs

1975. America as lost its war in Vietnam and Cambodia. Racially tinged riots are tearing the city of Boston apart. The politics and counterculture of the 1960s are disintegrating into nothing more than sex, drugs, and rock and roll. The Boston Red Sox are on one of their improbable runs toward a postseason appearance. In a suburban town in Maryland, a young couple are murdered and another young man is accused. The couple are white and the accused is black. It is up to his friends and family to prove he is innocent. This is a story of suburban ennui, race, murder, and injustice. Religion and politics, liberal lawyers and racist cops. In *Short Order Frame Up*, Ron Jacobs has written a piece of crime fiction that exposes the wound that is US racism. Two cultures existing side by side and across generations--a river very few dare to cross. His characters work and live with and next to each other, often unaware of each other's real life. When the murder occurs, however, those people that care about the man charged must cross that river and meet somewhere in between in order to free him from (what is to them) an obvious miscarriage of justice.

Loosestrife - Greg Delanty

This book is a chronicle of complicity in our modern lives, a witnessing of war and the destruction of our planet. It is also an attempt to adjust the more destructive blueprint myths of our society. Often our cultural memory tells us to keep quiet about the aspects that are most challenging to our ethics, to forget the violations we feel and tremors that keep us distant and numb.

When You Remember Deir Yassin - R. L. Green

"Robert Green's anguished poetry speaks with raw emotion, evoking the decades of conflict and intimate injustices between Arab and Jew in the land that is now Israel and Palestine. As a Jewish writer, Green is as familiar with the tragedy of the Nazi Holocaust as the massacre at Deir Yassin. He challenges his friends and family to open their hearts to the experiences of the people who bore the brunt of the Jewish catastrophe, the subsequent 'War of Liberation,' and the ongoing brutality of the Israeli occupation." – Alice Rothchild, MD, author of *Broken Promises, Broken Dreams: Stories of Jewish* and *Palestinian Trauma and Resilience*

Roadworthy Creature, Roadworthy Craft - Kate Magill

Words fail but the voice struggles on. The culmination of a decade's worth of performance poetry, *Roadworthy Creature, Roadworthy Craft* is Kate Magill's first full-length publication. In lines that are sinewy yet delicate, Magill's poems explore the terrain where idea and action meet, where bodies and words commingle to form a strange new flesh, a breathing text, an "I" that spirals outward from itself.

Entanglements - Tony Magistrale

A poet and a painter may employ different mediums to express the same snow-blown afternoon in January, but sometimes they find a way to capture the moment in such a way that their respective visions still manage to stir a reverberation, a connection. In part, that's what *Entanglements* seeks to do. Not so much for the poems and paintings to speak directly to one another, but for them to stir points of similarity.

Fomite
Burlington, VT

Visiting Hours - *Jennifer Anne Moses*
Visiting Hours, a novel-in-stories, explores the lives of people not normally met on the page——AIDS patients and those who care for them. Set in Baton Rouge, Louisiana, and written with large and frequent dollops of humor, the book is a profound meditation on faith and love in the face of illness and poverty.

The Listener Aspires to the Condition of Music - *Barry Goldensohn*
"I know of no other selected poems that selects on one theme, but this one does, charting Goldensohn's career-long attraction to music's performance, consolations and its august, thrilling, scary and clownish charms. Does all art aspire to the condition of music as Pater claimed, exhaling in a swoon toward that one class act? Goldensohn is more aware than the late 19th century of the overtones of such breathing: his poems thoroughly round out those overtones in a poet's lifetime of listening."
John Peck, poet, editor, Fellow of the American Academy of Rome

The Derivation of Cowboys & Indians - *Joseph D. Reich*
The Derivation of Cowboys & Indians represents a profound journey, a breakdown of the American Dream from a social, cultural, historical, and spiritual point of view. Reich examines in concise detail the loss of the collective unconscious, commenting on our contemporary postmodern culture with its self-interested excesses, on where and how things all go wrong, and how social/political practice rarely meets its original proclamations and promises. Reich's surreal and self-effacing satire brings this troubling message home. *The Derivation of Cowboys & Indians* is a desperate search and struggle for America's literal, symbolic, and spiritual home.

Views Cost Extra - L.E. Smith
Views that inspire, that calm, or that terrify—all come at some cost to the viewer. In *Views Cost Extra* you will find a New Jersey high school preppy who wants to inhabit the "perfect" cowboy movie, a rural mailman disgusted with the residents of his town who wants to live with the penguins, an ailing screen-writer who strikes a deal with Johnny Cash to reverse an old man's failures, an old man who ponders a young man's suicide attempt, a one-armed blind blues singer who wants to reunite with the car that took her arm on the assembly line—— and more. These stories suggest that we must pay something to live even ordinary lives.

Body of Work - Andrei Guruianu
Throughout thirteen stories, Body of Work chronicles the physical and emotional toll of characters consumed by the all-too-human need for a connection. Their world is achingly common — beauty and regret, obsession and self-doubt, the seductive charm of loneliness. Often fragmented, whimsical, always on the verge of melancholy, the collection is a sepia-toned portrait of nostalgia — each story like an artifact of our impermanence, an embrace of all that we have lost, of all that we might lose and love again someday.

Fomite
Burlington, VT

Travers' Inferno - *L.E. Smith*

In the 1970's, churches began to burn in Burlington, Vermont. If it was arson, no one or no reason could be found to blame. This book suggests arson, but makes no claim to historical realism. It claims, instead, to capture the dizzying 70's zeitgeist of aggressive utopian movements, distrust in authority, escapist alternative lifestyles, and a bewildered society of onlookers. In the tradition of John Gardner's *Sunlight Dialogues*, the characters of *Travers' Inferno* are colorful and damaged, sometimes comical, sometimes tragic, looking for meaning through desperate acts. Travers Jones, the protagonist, is grounded in the transcendent—philosophy, epilepsy, arson as purification—and mystified by the opposite sex, haunted by an absent father and directed by an uncle with a grudge. He is seduced by a professor's wife and chased by an endearing if ineffective sergeant of police. There are secessionist Quebecois involved in these church burns who are murdering as well as pilfering and burning. There are changing alliances, violent deaths, lovemaking, and a belligerent cat.

The Empty Notebook Interrogates Itself - Susan Thomas

The Empty Notebook began its life as a very literal metaphor for a few weeks of what the poet thought was writer's block, but was really the struggle of an eccentric persona to take over her working life. It won. And for the next three years everything she wrote came to her in the voice of the Empty Notebook, who, as the notebook began to fill itself, became rather opinionated, changed gender, alternately acted as bully and victim, had many bizarre adventures in exotic locales, and developed a somewhat politically incorrect attitude. It then began to steal the voices and forms of other poets and tried to immortalize itself in various poetry reviews. It is now thrilled to collect itself in one slim volume.

My God, What Have We Done? - Susan Weiss

In a world afflicted with war, toxicity, and hunger, does what we do in our private lives really matter? Fifty years after the creation of the atomic bomb at Los Alamos, newlyweds Pauline and Clifford visit that once-secret city on their honeymoon, compelled by Pauline's fascination with Oppenheimer, the soulful scientist. The two stories emerging from this visit reverberate back and forth between the loneliness of a new mother at home in Boston and the isolation of an entire community dedicated to the development of the bomb. While Pauline struggles with unforeseen challenges of family life, Oppenheimer and his crew reckon with forces beyond all imagining. Finally the years of frantic research on the bomb culminate in a stunning test explosion that echoes a rupture in the couple's marriage. Against the backdrop of a civilization that's out of control, Pauline begins to understand the complex, potentially explosive physics of personal relationships. At once funny and dead serious, *My God, What Have We Done?* sifts through the ruins left by the bomb in search of a more worthy human achievement.

Suite for Three Voices - *Derek Furr*

Suite for Three Voices is a dance of prose genres, teeming with intense human life in all its humor and sorrow. A son uncovers the horrors of his father's wartime experience, a hitchhiker in a muumuu guards a mysterious parcel, a young man foresees his brother's brush with death on September 11. A Victorian poetess encounters space aliens and digital archives, a runner hears the voice of a dead friend in the song of an indigo bunting, a teacher seeks wisdom from his students' errors and Neil Young. By frozen waterfalls and neglected graveyards, along highways at noon and rivers at dusk, in the sound of bluegrass, Beethoven, and Emily Dickinson, the essays and fiction in this collection offer moments of vision.

Fomite
Burlington, VT

As It Is On Earth - Peter M. Wheelwright

Four centuries after the Reformation Pilgrims sailed up the down-flowing watersheds of New England, Taylor Thatcher, irreverent scion of a fallen family of Maine Puritans, is still caught in the turbulence. In his errant attempts to escape from history, the young college professor is further unsettled by his growing attraction to Israeli student Miryam Bluehm as he is swept by Time through the "family thing"—from the tangled genetic and religious history of his New England parents to the redemptive birthday secret of Esther Fleur Noire Bishop, the Cajun-Passamaquoddy woman who raised him and his younger half-cousin/half-brother, Bingham.The landscapes, rivers, and tidal estuaries of Old New England and the Mayan Yucatan are also casualties of history in Thatcher's story of Deep Time and re-discovery of family on Columbus Day at a high-stakes gambling casino, rising in resurrection over the starlit bones of a once-vanquished Pequot Indian tribe.

Love's Labours - Jack Pulaski

In the four stories and two novellas that comprise *Love's Labors* the protagonists, Ben and Laura, discover in their fervid romance and long marriage their interlocking fates, and the histories that preceded their births. They also learned something of the paradox between love and all the things it brings to its beneficiaries: bliss, disaster, duty, tragedy, comedy, the grotesque, and tenderness. Ben and Laura's story is also the particularly American tale of immigration to a new world. Laura's story begins in Puerto Rico, and Ben's lineage is Russian-Jewish. They meet in City College of New York, a place at least analogous to a melting pot. Laura struggles to rescue her brother from gang life and heroin. She is mother to her younger sister; their mother Consuelo is the financial mainstay of the family and consumed by work. Despite filial obligations, Laura aspires to be a serious painter. Ben writes, cares for, and is caught up in the misadventures and surreal stories of his younger schizophrenic brother. Laura is also a story teller as powerful and enchanting as Scheherazade. Ben struggles to survive such riches, and he and Laura endure.

Signed Confessions - Tom Walker

Guilt and a desperate need to repent drive the antiheroes in Tom Walker's dark (and often darkly funny) stories: a gullible journalist falls for the 40-year-old stripper he profiles in a magazine, a faithless husband abandons his family and joins a support group for lost souls., a merciless prosecuting attorney grapples with the suicide of his gay son, an aging misanthrope must make amends to five former victims, an egoistic naval hero is haunted by apparitions of his dead wife and a mysterious little girl.The seven tales in *Signed Confessions* measure how far guilty men will go to obtain a forgiveness no one can grant but themselves.

Screwed – Stephen Goldberg

Screwed is a collection of five plays by Stephen Goldberg, who has written over twenty-five produced plays and is co-founder of the Off Center or the Dramatic Arts in Burlington, Vermont.

Fomite
Burlington, VT

The Housing Market - Joseph D. Reich

In Joseph Reich's most recent social and cultural, contemporary satire of suburbia entitled, "The Housing market: a comfortable place to jump off the end of the world," the author addresses the absurd, postmodern elements of what it means, or for that matter not, to try and cope and function, and survive and thrive, or live and die in the repetitive and existential, futile and self-destructive, homogenized, monochromatic landscape of a brutal and bland, collective unconscious, which can spiritually result in a gradual wasting away and erosion of the senses or conflict and crisis of a desperate, disproportionate 'situational depression,' triggering and leading the narrator to feel constantly abandoned and stranded, more concretely or proverbially spoken, "the eternal stranger," where when caught between the fight or flight psychological phenomena, naturally repels him and causes him to flee and return without him even knowing it into the wild, while by sudden circumstance and coincidence discovers it surrounds the illusory-like circumference of these selfsame Monopoly board cul-de-sacs and dead ends. Most specifically, what can happen to a solitary, thoughtful, and independent thinker when being stagnated in the triangulation of a cookie-cutter, oppressive culture of a homeowner's association; a memoir all written in critical and didactic, poetic stanzas and passages, and out of desperation, when freedom and control get taken, what he is forced to do in the illusion of 'free will and volition,' something like the derivative art of a smart and ironic and social and cultural satire.

Still Time - Michael Cocchiarale

Still Time is a collection of twenty-five short and shorter stories exploring tensions that arise in a variety of contemporary relationships: a young boy must deal with the wrath of his out-of-work father; a woman runs into a man twenty years after an awkward sexual encounter; a wife, unable to conceive, imagines her own murder, as well as the reaction of her emotionally distant husband; a soon-to-be-tenured English professor tries to come to terms with her husband's shocking return to the religion of his youth; an assembly line worker, married for thirty years, discovers the surprising secret life of his recently hospitalized wife. Whether a few hundred or a few thousand words, these and other stories in the collection depict characters at moments of deep crisis. Some feel powerless, overwhelmed—unable to do much to change the course of their lives. Others rise to the occasion and, for better or for worse, say or do the thing that might transform them for good. Even in stories with the most troubling of endings, there remains the possibility of redemption. For each of the characters, there is still time.

Raven or Crow - Joshua Amses

Marlowe has recently moved back home to Vermont after flunking his first term at a private college in the Midwest, when his sort-of girlfriend, Eleanor, goes missing. The circumstances surrounding Eleanor's disappearance stand to reveal more about Marlowe than he is willing to allow. Rather than report her missing, he resolves to find Eleanor himself. *Raven or Crow* is the story of mistakes rooted in the ambivalence of being young and without direction.

Fomite
Burlington, VT

The Good Muslim of Jackson Heights - Jaysinh Birjépatil

Jackson Heights in this book is a fictional locale with common features assembled from immigrant-friendly neighborhoods around the world where hardworking honest-to-goodness traders from the Indian subcontinent rub shoulders with ruthless entrepreneurs, reclusive antique-dealers, homeless nobodies, merchant-princes, lawyers, doctors, and IT specialists. But as Siraj and Shabnam, urbane newcomers fleeing religious persecution in their homeland, discover, there is no escape from the past. Weaving together the personal and the political. *The Good Muslim of Jackson Heights* is an ambiguous elegy to a utopian ideal set free from all prejudice.

Meanwell - Janice Miller Potter

Meanwell is a twenty-four-poem sequence in which a female servant searches for identity and meaning in the shadow of her mistress, poet Anne Bradstreet. Although Meanwell herself is a fiction, someone like her could easily have existed among Bradstreet's known but unnamed domestic servants. Through Meanwell's eyes, Bradstreet emerges as a human figure during the Great Migration of the 1600s, a period in which the Massachusetts Bay Colony was fraught with physical and political dangers. Through Meanwell, the feelings of women, silenced during the midwife Anne Hutchinson's fiery trial before the Puritan ministers, are finally acknowledged. In effect, the poems are about the making of an American rebel. Through her conflicted conscience, we witness Meanwell's transformation from a powerless English waif to a mythic American who ultimately chooses wilderness over the civilization she has experienced.

Four-Way Stop - Sherry Olson

If *Thank You* were the only prayer, as Meister Eckhart has suggested, it would be enough, and Sherry Olson's poetry, in her second book, *Four-Way Stop*, would be one. Radical attention, deep love, and dedication to kindness illuminate these poems and the stories she tells us, which are drawn from her own life: with family, with friends, and wherever she travels, with strangers – who to Olson, never are strangers, but kin. Even at the difficult intersections, as in the title poem, *Four-Way Stop*, Olson experiences – and offers – hope, showing us how, *completely unsupervised*, people take turns, with *kindness waving each other on*. Olson writes, knowing that (to quote Czeslaw Milosz) *What surrounds us, here and now, is not guaranteed*. To this world, with her poems, Olson brings – and teaches – attention, generosity, compassion, and appreciative joy. —Carol Henrikson

Dons of Time - Greg Guma

"Wherever you look...there you are." The next media breakthrough has just happened. They call it Remote Viewing and Tonio Wolfe is at the center of the storm. But the research underway at TELPORT's off-the-books lab is even more radical -- opening a window not only to remote places but completely different times. Now unsolved mysteries are colliding with cutting edge science and altered states of consciousness in a world of corporate gangsters, infamous crimes and top-secret experiments. Based on eyewitness accounts, suppressed documents and the lives of world-changers like Nikola Tesla, Annie Besant and Jack the Ripper, Dons of Time is a speculative adventure, a glimpse of an alternative future and a quantum leap to Gilded Age London at the tipping point of invention, revolution and murder.

Fomite
Burlington, VT

Alfabestiario
AlphaBetaBestiario - Antonello Borra

Animals have always understood that mankind is not fully at home in the world. Bestiaries, hoping to teach, send out warnings. This one, of course, aims at doing the same.

The Consequence of Gesture - *L.E. Smith*

On a Monday evening in December of 1980, Mark David Chapman murdered John Lennon outside his apartment building in New York City. The Consequence of Gesture brings the reader along a three-day countdown to mayhem. This book inserts Chapman into the weekend plans of a group of friends sympathetic with his obsession to shatter a cultural icon and determined to perform their own iconoclastic gestures. John Lennon's life is not the only one that hangs in the balance. No one will emerge the same.

Sinfonia Bulgarica—Zdravka Evtimova

Sinfonia Bulgarica is a novel about four women in contemporary Bulgaria: a rich cold-blooded heiress, a masseuse dreaming of peace and quiet that never come, a powerful wife of the most influential man in the country, and a waitress struggling against all odds to win a victory over lies, poverty and humiliation. It is a realistic book of vice and yearning, of truthfulness and schemes, of love and desperation. The heroes are plain-spoken characters, whose action is limited by the contradictions of a society where lowness rules at many levels. The novel draws a picture of life in a country where many people believe that "Money is the most loyal friend of man". Yet the four women have an even more loyal friend: ruthlessness of life.

My Father's Keeper - Andrew Potok

The turmoil, terror and betrayal of their escape from Poland at the start of World War II lead us into this tale of hatred and forgiveness between father and son.

Unfinished Stories of Girls—Catherine Zobal Dent

The sixteen stories in this debut collection set on the Eastern Shore of Maryland feature powerfully drawn characters with troubles and subjects such as communal guilt over a drunk-driving car accident that kills a young girl, the doomed marriage of a jewelry clerk and an undercover cop, the obsessions of a housecleaner jailed for forging her employers' signatures, the heart-breaking closeness of a family stuck in the snow. Each of Unfinished Stories of Girls' richly textured tales is embedded in the quiet and sometimes violent fields, towns, and riverbeds that are the backdrop for life in tidewater Maryland. Dent's deep love for her region shines through, but so does her melancholic thoughtfulness about its challenges and problems. The reader is invited inside the lives of characters trying to figure out the marshy world around them, when that world leaves much up to the imagination

Fomite
Burlington, VT

The Hundred Yard Dash Man - Barry Goldensohn

In dedicating this volume of poetry to his father, who was a championship runner in his time, Goldensohn compares the lyric poem to the hundred yard dash. Fans of Goldensohn's work will find poems chosen from previous published works, including *St. Venus Eve, Uncarving the Block, The Marrano, Dance Music* and *East Long Pond*, as well as a generous portion of new work.

The Moment Before An Injury - Joshua Amses

At a glance, Acheron, Vermont contains all the people you expect to meet in an average New England college town. The bumbling, corrupt Sheriff Blivet, and his son Purvis, a junior paranormal investigator. Wilbur Broom, an alcoholic cine-phile with a tragic past, and transfer student Denise, his mysterious and bewitch-ing niece. And of course, local real estate magnate Joshua Castle, and his much younger, and far more ruthless wife, Jo. They all have secrets, and who better to compile them than Henry Hoffmann, blackmailer, tour guide, and adviser to Mr. Castle. In these capacities, Henry enjoys unlimited power and influence over the citizens of Acheron, until several strange events the week before Halloween put him at the mercy of the very people it is his job to control. The Moment Before an Injury is a novel of amoral ghosts, stolen dogs, creative revenge, petty criminality, vocational ennui, and the fragile politics of absolute power in a small town.

Cycling in Plato's Cave - David Cavanagh

How we relate, how we know what we think we know, how past mingles with present, how a bike stays upright, how the butt can bear that puny perch – a lot more than pedals and wheels goes around in Cycling in Plato's Cave. Just like a bike, the poems are simple but have deftly moving parts that roll us along, offer fresh perspectives, and let us feel the air. And just like on a sunny Sunday in June, or is it September, or maybe it's cloudy and broody outside, it's all about the ride.

When You Remember Deir Yassin - R. L. Green

"Robert Green's anguished poetry speaks with raw emotion, evoking the decades of conflict and intimate injustices between Arab and Jew in the land that is now Israel and Palestine. As a Jewish writer, Green is as familiar with the tragedy of the Nazi Holocaust as the massacre at Deir Yassin. He challenges his friends and family to open their hearts to the experiences of the people who bore the brunt of the Jewish catastrophe, the subsequent 'War of Liberation,' and the ongoing brutality of the Israeli occupation." – Alice Rothchild, MD, author of *Broken Promises, Broken Dreams: Stories of Jewish* and *Palestinian Trauma and Resilience*

Drawing on Life - Mason Drukman

Mason Drukman's collection—augmented by the artistry of Lisa Esherick—of-fers a fresh poetic voice that speaks with intelligence, clarity, humor and heart. His subject matter is life itself: culture, politics, family, death, grief, love and the Red Sox. Welcome to his special kind of poetry.

Fomite

Burlington, VT

CPSIA information can be obtained at www.ICGtesting.com
Printed in the USA
LVOW13s0011210814

400191LV00001B/160/P

9 781937 677787